P9-DUH-667

Her
Kind
of
Want

The

Iowa

Short

Fiction

Award

University of

Iowa Press

Iowa City

Jennifer S. Davis

Her Kind of Want

University of Iowa Press, Iowa City 52242

Copyright © 2002 by Jennifer S. Davis

All rights reserved

Printed in the United States of America

http://www.uiowa.edu/uiowapress

No part of this book may be reproduced or used in any form
or by any means without permission in writing from the
publisher. All reasonable steps have been taken to contact
copyright holders of material used in this book. The publisher
would be pleased to make suitable arrangements with any
whom it has not been possible to reach. This is a work of
fiction; any resemblance to actual events or persons is entirely
coincidental.

Printed on acid-free paper

The publication of this book was generously supported by the
University of Iowa Foundation and the National Endowment
for the Arts.

Library of Congress Cataloging-in-Publication Data

Davis, Jennifer S., 1973–

    Her kind of want / Jennifer S. Davis.

       p.   cm.—(The Iowa short fiction award)

       Contents: Rewriting girl: an introduction—The ballad
of my father's redneck wife—Some things collide—Only
ends—What kind of man—The one thing God'll give
you—PoJo's and the buttery slope—Tammy, imagined—
When you see.

    ISBN 0-87745-818-9 (pbk.)

       1. United States—Social life and customs—20th
century—Fiction. I. Title. II. Series.

PS3604.A96 H47 2002

813'.6—dc21   2002018061

02   03   04   05   06   P   5   4   3   2   1

For my parents,

Joe and Lois Davis,

and my grandparents,

Helen and Harvey Davis,

who taught me to always remember

from where I come

I have found the warm caves in the woods,

filled them with skillets, carvings, shelves,

closets, silks, innumerable goods;

fixed the suppers for the worms and the elves:

whining, rearranging the disaligned.

A woman like that is misunderstood.

I have been her kind.

—ANNE SEXTON

from "Her Kind"

Contents

ACKNOWLEDGMENTS

I feel blessed to have come from Alabama,
to have known the wonderful people of my
home, to have listened to their stories and the
stories of the landscape. My family has been
unbelievably supportive all these years (even
if they sometimes questioned if I belonged to
them), and I appreciate their understanding
and respect for the different choices I have
made. Thanks to my Aunt Pat for her moral
support. Thanks to my brother Scott, who
taught me to run trotlines and train bird
dogs, and to my brother Alan, who took me
mud hopping when I couldn't see over the
dash. They gave me the mythology of my
childhood, which continues to feed me today.
A special thanks to Deirdre McNamer, who was
the first person to have faith in my writing.
The students and teachers at the MFA
program at the University of Alabama were
extremely supportive, and I am deeply
indebted to Dr. Phillip Beidler, Michael
Martone, and Dr. Wendy Rawlings for their
help with my manuscript.
Thanks to Hilary Funk and Bebe Barefoot, who
keep me sane, to Geoff Trumbo, who edited
my work tirelessly, and to Charley Henley,
who convinced me to write what I know and
then took the time to read it.
I owe a special debt to the University of Iowa
Press for giving new writers a chance to get
their work out into the world. They've been
unbelievably kind.
I thank God that I have been fortunate enough
to have such lovely people touch my life.

Rewriting Girl

An Introduction

―――――――
████████

Sean wrote stories of snapping beans on the front porch of his grandma's house in Eufaula, Alabama. Not only a porch, but a built-on porch of an eaten-out double-wide cluttered with catsup packets and faded pink Sweet 'n Lows and plastic knives and forks and the Styrofoam bottoms from hamburger meat because they might be needed someday and you never know. The poorer and dirtier the better. He'd write poems and stories and plays about the South and his Southern and grandmas and snapping beans, and I knew he was really from Philadelphia but had lived with his grandmother for a summer when he was eight or so, old enough to just remember the outlines of something. I didn't know how to tell him that wearing a fishing lure in your ear like he tended to do isn't tacky redneck, but just tacky, and Southern is a hard life you didn't want to acquire.

And me. Fresh from Tallassee, fresh from working at the Hardee's drive-through and giving all the high school boys free sweet teas or a large fry for the price of a small. Them waiting out front closing time revving motors of old cars, eaten out like I think Sean wanted his grandma's remembered trailer to be, and us driving around town sipping Milwaukee's Best and choking on cigarettes and Led Zeppelin and bad dope. Me half-naked and tight-nippled on the boat landing out behind Mr. Radley's fishing shack, and old Radley trying to scare us by flashing the deer-blinding lights and shooting guns into sky filled with the stars the boys said were nothing compared to my eyes. Sneaking in the oh-God-I-hope-Momma-don't-wake-up quiet kitchen door, and her sitting there drinking coffee black, European-like she said, in tiny flowered china cups we ordered from *Good Housekeeping* when I was little enough to still be girl. Momma tired of serving fake blushed smiles and attitude to deadened workers and wannabe cowboys down at the Rodeo Club, her tired of mothering me and my growing mouth and fleshing body. Her tired. And as always, I said, Yes, I was a good girl, Momma, when she asked, as she always asked, and she was so tired, my momma, and Southern is a hard life to acquire.

When I woke up with Ralph gone in the $19.99-a-night motel and mountains eating the space of my window and cold around me blanketed, I thought of being scared, but was hungry. So I made sure Ralph hadn't taken off with the money I always tape to my thigh like my momma taught me and her momma taught her and walked the few blocks to the Hardee's and asked for a steak biscuit, add cheese please, but they don't have steak biscuits at the Hardee's in Montana in spite of all the cows, and that was the beginning of what I thought would be different. My hair was long and black and romantic then, and made boys and men feel like boys and men when it rippled and pooled behind me. And I walked around in the spring morning nibbling my breakfast in the blanketed cold and saw the clean kind of hippies, the don't-have-to-be-hippies kind of hippies, although I didn't know the difference at the time, beating drums and gyrating under the bridge. One called out, Hey hippie girl, and I blushed, dimpled, and told them I wasn't no hippie but Little Hula, fresh from Tallassee, Alabama. And my pooling, rippling hair and pooling, rippling accent reminded them they were boys and men and it wasn't two hours before I had myself a place to stay. That's how life is for me and I hope that don't make me the bad kind of girl.

Later, after I met Sean at the coffeehouse where I worked and he wrote his stories about grandmas and snapping beans on the built-on porch to the double-wide, I told him about Ralph, and him dating Momma and her not so tired for once and smiling. Ralph, goateed and earringed and work hardened in that sexy way Clint Eastwood pretends to be. And the day he slid his hand down my back while she was at work and me not understanding and this time allowing it to go in full belly instead of spewing warm and stunted on my stomach like the other boys, and Momma walking in and seeing him hulking between my spread-open thighs and her no longer able to pretend I'm girl. Her throwing those flowered china teacups ordered out of *Good Housekeeping* right at Ralph's goateed face and calling me a bitch slut, although I know she didn't mean it cause I know now Ralph's nothing to lose your girl over. And her kicking us both out and me riding across smooth burlaped country to rolling mountains in Ralph's truck until I woke up in Montana with my money, thank God, still taped to my thigh and Ralph and his truck gone. I told Sean this, and how I hoped to go home and see Momma soon, maybe after I'd gotten myself an education at the university, maybe in theater, maybe I'd be a wonderful actress with my rippling, pooling hair that makes boys and men remember they're boys and men, and then Momma could quit working at the Rodeo Club and quit being so tired. I told him this and all else I know, Momma and her tinkling-bell laughter like all-year Christmas, and Little Orphan Annie stories whispered on her night-tired breath, and azalea bushes dripping blooms in our front yard, and the liver shape of my favorite ledge sliding into sky, and standing on top of Ralph's boot-weighted feet skating over the kitchen floor to Willie's *Angel Flying Too Close to the Ground*, when Ralph was still hope and I was still girl, before I let it go in full belly instead of spewing warm and stunted on my stomach. And Sean rubbed my hand and kised me and told me my life was a stereotype, a cliché, and when he wrote me he'd write me differently, maybe without the Hardee's and the waitress momma and Ralph hulking between my spread-open thighs, that he might write those things but paint me in a different light. Do I get to be the hero? I asked.

Sean had money, although he liked to pretend that he didn't, like the hippies-who-didn't-have-to-be-hippies who played drums in a circle and gyrated under the bridge liked to pretend they didn't in order to make their old stories or potential stories better. But I know not having money and it's not a good story, and Sean had it, and maybe I stayed with him for it, and I hope that doesn't make me the bad kind of girl. He'd buy me short black silky dresses, the kind Momma would wear to catch hope like Ralph but never let me wear, the kind I'd sneak out of her closet to dance tight-nippled on old Radley's boat landing. Sean would dress me in those short black silky dresses with knee-high boots against the blanketed cold bought secondhand at vintage shops playing loud music with cashiers in rhinestoned movie-star glasses and platform shoes because Sean was the kind who paid for worn. And I'd wear his dresses and his boots and my hair down, and he'd wear me and take me to parties with people who looked like the cashiers at the vintage stores, where they would discuss Russian authors and summer trips to India and Africa and ask each other what they'd read. He'd make me memorize the names of books by men named Tolstoy and Dostoevsky, and I tried not to confuse who wrote what but I always did, and I think that's what he wanted me to do anyway. And everyone swayed into my thick, rippling accent and pretended not to notice when I confused, but cringed their sucked-in long faces and *hmmmed* me, and after a while I just quit talking and Sean talked for me.

On Friday nights his people would meet at the coffeehouse where I worked and Sean wrote stories about snapping beans on his grandma's built-on porch, and they would sip wine and drink expensive beers, although everyone said no one had money. One or the other would climb to the dim-lighted front and stand behind a podium where they'd read stories about depressed writers or people who were depressed because they wanted to be writers or summer trips to India or Africa in smooth, trained voices, stopping to sip water or whiskey and clearing their throats, and everyone pretending to listen and watch but really rewriting their own stories in their heads or thinking they could write someone else's story better.

My last night with Sean he eased behind that dim-lighted podium with his tacky fishing lure hanging from his ear, me sitting and watching in my black dress and boots against the blanketed cold, and he told the story of a redneck girl from Alabama who works at Hardee's and lets boys and men feel her up on the boat landing, and her unknowing, open and easy and wanting instead of reading books and knowing authors' names. He wrote her momma tragic, as the dried-up whore her daughter is destined to become, with boyfriends who roll through both of them like open fields, like the open burlaped fields I crossed coming to those mountains that ate up my window. And that's how he ended us, opened and gnawed out and empty, with Southern a hard life you didn't want to acquire.

When he finished everyone clapped politely, thinking how they could have written it better, and I eased my long hair proper-like behind my ears, my long hair that reminded boys and men that they're boys and men, my long hair that reminded me of the women we are. And I thought of all he didn't write. Momma and her lovely china cups ordered from *Good Housekeeping* when I was girl. Her tinkling-bell laughter like all-year Christmas. The azaleas dripping blooms with pink flesh skin as soft as my momma's cheek when she pressed it against mine and whispered Little Orphan Annie stories on night-tired breath. The French fries and sweet teas and the sweeter boys who danced their bodies against mine under the stars they said were nothing compared to my eyes. And Ralph before, work hardened but kind, skating me around the kitchen on boot-weighted feet, a skin-scabbed hand against my back to steady me with no thought to slide it down and take Momma's hope. And me standing against blanketed cold smiling at the hippies-who-don't-have-to-be-hippies, me rippling and blushing and dimpling in a new old world, but me still standing and seeing. Sean rewrote me without writing me at all, and still everyone offered a *clap clap clap* and *ahhhhed* his story of me with the same mouths that *hmmmed* me at parties. And everyone thinking that all girls like me are the bad kind of girls who make good stories to sigh over dim-lighted podiums or at parties under the hum about books by men named Tolstoy and Dostoevsky.

So I slipped from the coffee shop while Sean was being *pat pat patted* on the back for a fine piece of work, people flowing praise into his tacky redneck fishing-lure ear, and I walked to his apartment where I stayed to get my things, passing the don't-have-to-be-hippie hippies beating drums and gyrating under the wide sky by the bridge. One called out, Hey hippie girl, and I smiled, flashing my pooling, rippling hair and pooling, rippling accent and told them I wasn't no hippie but Little Hula, from Tallassee, Alabama. My black short silky dress whispering bitter against my thighs, my knee-high boots not doing much against the cold, and me thinking that the sky and the stars in Montana are the same ones the boys at home said were nothing compared to my eyes, only somehow clearer. Closer.

The Ballad
of My Father's
Redneck Wife

Her name is Bebe Hicks.

The name of a rodeo queen, perhaps. Blonde curls under the squeeze of a Stetson. Or a Miss Something Obscure—maybe Miss Azalea Festival or Miss Apple Blossom Jubilee. A hand curved into a wave. A mouth curved into an almost-smile. These were my first thoughts.

Let me clarify.

This isn't some story about a man with a dual existence, a form of simulacrum if you will: a home with a wife and two kids and a dog in one suburb, a home with a wife and two kids and a dog in another, matching suits hanging in both closets, the wives with identical nicknames to eliminate confusion in intimate moments or when jostled from a daydream. This is not a story about the kind of men you hear about on talk shows; the wives, always shadows of each other, staring in awe at the woman/women leading her same life, or possibly a better version of it. *But he massaged my feet, ran my bath,* one woman might say. *He taught my dyslexic son how to read, made me spinach ravioli and tiramisu by candlelight once a month,* another whimpers. A smooth-talking man in an orange uniform via satellite from a low-security prison shrugging broad shoulders, his eyes lazy and blue like daytime TV. You thinking, *I would have known better. I would have seen the signs.*

Bebe Hicks was my father's first wife, the one before my mother, the one before he became the man I know as my father. Before the education, before the money, before the Mercedes, before the exotic vacations, before the annoyingly esoteric vocabulary. Before his parents died and he left his hometown of Waynesville and never went back.

Bebe Hicks. My other possible mother.

But I would have dimples and blonde hair instead of black frizz and freckles. I would be skinny and wiry without starving myself. I might drink whiskey and smoke menthols and say things like Honey and Darlin and Sweetheart with a voice riding velvet. Have torrid relationships with men in snakeskin cowboy hats and five-day stubble, men who stand outside my window howling in agony because I said it would never work. The other me. The sexy me. The possibly better me.

I know what you might think. Many men have been married more than once. Many fathers have ex-wives. What's the big deal?

And I guess there isn't one, except to say, most fathers don't wait until you're thirty-two and wiping the Thanksgiving stuffing off your one-year-old's chin for you to find out from your Aunt Claudine that he was married for almost three years once before, to a woman other than your mother, to a woman from Waynesville, Alabama, named Bebe Hicks.

My mother once told me, on the night of my senior prom, the night I waited on the bench in our foyer for two hours in a garishly purple organza gown I chose specifically to insult my mother, the night I got stood up by the man I knew was destined as my soul mate—the man who wore a black leather coat like some men pack heat, the man who flipped me on my back for the first time with a flick of his finger under my chin and a wry smile—that there was one secret to domestic happiness. Make sure your husband loves you far more than you love him, but you have to like him a little.

Like and *little* are the key words here.

I married Mike Hilbert the real estate agent, who studied business at the University of Alabama, who wears plaid shirts and khakis, loafers with leather fringe on the top. I stay at home and take care of Allie. We go to Destin for vacation. Eat at Applebee's and O'Charley's. He orders steak medium well and I get the grilled chicken and my salad dressing on the side. On Friday nights we hire a babysitter and see a romantic comedy with simple characters and plots we forget on the silent ride home where I pretend to fall asleep on the couch and Mike pretends it isn't intentional.

When asked, I say, "My husband, he's a good man."

I like him a little less than I should.

My sister Amanda doesn't like anyone, but she'll sleep with anybody.

I suspect my mother thinks my father likes her more than he does.

After Thanksgiving dinner my Aunt Claudine told me, in private, that my father was crazy for Bebe, that he got in fistfights if someone looked her way, and everyone looked her way. That he spray-painted I LOVE YOU BEBE across her sidewalk, got himself arrested and his picture in the local paper, received probation and community service. That he did it again.

But I get ahead of myself.

My father: gray suits, silver hair, a scotch in the afternoons, an appreciation for Mozart's Requiem and Ayn Rand, smokes a cigar on occasion, speaks softly but with purpose, runs five miles a day, drinks carrot juice he hates because it's good for him, plays racquetball every Saturday morning, golf on Sunday afternoons, buys my mother a new diamond tennis bracelet each Christmas, started an engineering firm at thirty after earning a degree from Georgia Tech, buys Mercedes, but never the top-of-the-line luxury series, hugs when appropriate.

My mother: skin and clothing various shades of cream/beige, holds a martini but never finishes it, studied art history at the University of Georgia and offers witty anecdotes about Picasso and Van Gogh, never worked a job that pays, heads two book clubs and the town welcoming committee, spent years eradicating the words (still a debate as to whether or not they are indeed words) *ain't* and *fixen* from my sister's and my vocabulary, hugs when appropriate.

Aunt Claudine is my father's younger sister. She still lives in Waynesville but has a condo in Orange Beach and a townhouse in Montgomery. She married a local boy, Bodine, who likes to bass-fish (won Bass Masters Mr. Bass last year, which was treated with more reverence than their daughter's graduation from the university) and flies to Argentina each spring to bird-hunt. By a fluke chain of events, Bodine inherited his great-uncle's car rental company (one of the bigger names) and sold it a few years later for millions. Claudine has black feathered hair that rivals Cher's and an affinity for gold and silver shoes, sings throaty songs about dog-dirty men while walking through the mall or the grocery, and recently dried out, though her sobriety is hard to discern.

I've seen my aunt about five times in my life, although she lives relatively close. My father rarely invites her over, doesn't like reminders of his upbringing. But this particular Thanksgiving she showed up at my parents' door with her entire brood.

Here's how it happened: My mother was in the kitchen preparing more water-chestnut stuffing, my father was sipping a scotch, and my sister was snipping at her husband (her fourth) for his plate of food, which was massive, as she has a passionate dislike for anyone else's gluttony.

Myself, tired of making up excuses as to why Mike hadn't come, was attempting to coax Allie to eat. Like many idiots before us, Mike and I thought Allie would cement our relationship. Ever since Mike and I started having problems, Allie, who unfortunately takes after Mike's side of the family in the looks category, had become a finicky eater. Her face lacked the rosiness of the Gerber babies I so coveted as proof of my maternal abilities, abilities I was convinced I lacked because I thought of such things in the first place.

Bodine was three sheets to the wind and sucking on turkey

bones, encouraging his boy Wilton to make statues out of his mashed potatoes. Their daughter Cindy, who'd recently discovered the concept of starving herself, pushed around some lettuce and green beans on her plate with disturbingly skeletal fingers. And Aunt Claudine, who was on her second pack of Virginia Slim menthols (one vice at a time she said), had finished her third plate and looked thoroughly bored.

After a few minutes of silence and chewing, Aunt Claudine blurted out to my father, "Hey, you ever talk to that Hicks girl, the one you were so crazy about?"

My sister Amanda, thinking Aunt Claudine had said "that hick girl" and always up for a bit of gossip, said, "What hick girl, Dad?"

Aunt Claudine let out a laugh that sounded more like a belch and said, "Good God, Bebe Hicks, your daddy's first wife."

My sister squealed in delight. Her husband reached for a roll. Wilton slammed his fork against his potato alien statue. I heard silverware drop in the kitchen where my mother was hiding. Allie started wailing, smearing stuffing on her high chair.

"Wife?" I said.

"That lounge singer. She was a wild one," Uncle Bodine said gravelly and low, like he had firsthand knowledge

My father sipped his scotch, raised an eyebrow, quietly said, "That's enough," his voice, somehow, as always, a slap.

For those of you with inanimate, frigid parents, parents whose voices or temperatures rarely flare, you will understand why this was such an important development. You will understand what years of quiet voices and cool hugs and cutting looks can do to a woman, what that kind of environment breeds, what you are left with.

———

Sitting on our marriage counselor's Swedish leather couch, I was asked to make a list of the things that irritate me about my husband. It went more or less like this:

Wears geeky khaki shorts
Tries to monopolize our daughter's affections
Refuses to cut toenails/nose hair

Breathes heavy even after I ask him to stop
Expects too much sex / likes strange positions
Plays loud music and sings along after I ask him to stop
Too many self-referential conversations about his own feelings
Touches inappropriately in public
Gawks at women's breasts
Chews with mouth open / puts food in mouth before previous
food is swallowed

His is a bit easier to sum up. I am a bitch.
I'd cut him off.
My label is "emotionally distant."
A few weeks after Thanksgiving, in one of our private sessions,
I asked the therapist if there was such a diagnosis as "terminal
bore," and if so, could she be sure to put that on Mike's record.
She said I had issues with intimacy.
"I hate him," I said.
"I see," she said, scribbling something on her notepad.
"What do you want?" she asked.
"Passion," I said.
"And how would you define that?"
This is what I thought: My father crazed, rabid, throwing his
thin body against Bebe Hicks's front door, threatening to end his
life if she didn't talk, just talk to him.
"I don't know," I said.
Late at night, when I was pregnant with Allie, Mike would
sometimes lay his head on my belly, splay his hand against my
heart. It's weight, so heavy. Once he said, "Do you know how
much I could love you, Jill? But I just don't feel you trying."
There are many ways to avoid the threat of love.
My sister gorges on sex. Thus all the husbands. When we were
teenagers any man who came near the house was in danger of
seduction. The postman. The cable guy. The summer my parents
added on a sunroom and there were workers all around, my sister
was on her back more often than not. She would stomp through
the front door after her dates, her bra hanging from her purse, her
stockings torn, and plop down on the couch beside my mother,
who never sleeps but never looks tired, waiting. My mother would
tuck her knees to her chest, rearrange her afghan, ask my sister,

"Did you have a nice time?" and go back to doing nothing with great focus.

"The problem with your sister," my mother once said, "is that she is in love with love." She said this as if being in love with love was the most wretched state a woman could enter.

Amanda has her own explanation of her problems with men. She says my mother had an affair when we were teenagers, a charge I don't believe, an Amanda truth unearthed in hypnosis therapy.

My mother and the next-door neighbor.

She says she saw them writhing naked in the pool when she ditched school one afternoon. Mother's breasts buoyant. His sunburned, furry back looming. Certainly this was the cause of her distaste for the masculine form. Amanda seemed very pleased to have the information at the time, hugged it to her, slept with it, wallowed in it. She refused to confront my mother.

"Dr. Ellen says this is about me, not Mother," she told me over martinis one night at a local bar. "She says it's important to know the source of my problems with intimacy." She'd just frosted her hair and started tanning. Husband number two was on his way out. A new man in the works.

"We learn how to love from our parents," she said, leaning closer, the whites of her eyes bulbous, too white against her electric blue liner. "Your family, it explains *everything*."

Amanda's my baby sister. At one time, I wanted her dancing in daisies. Babies under each arm. A content smile. The things we want for our sisters while wrapping ourselves in gauzy white drapes as children, playing wedding, taking turns being the groom, being the bride. Now I want her sober. Her husbands off my front porch at all hours of the night, beating on my door while I hide in the shadows. "I know you know where that bitch is" echoing against the concrete of suburbia.

Within an hour Amanda downed two more martinis, picked up a guy at the bar, whispered for me to tell her husband the usual if he called.

Amanda breaks all of our hearts.

"Goes to show what they always say," Mike said later that evening when I told him about my mother. We were engaged at the time. "You never know what people have in their closets."

I tried to think of something raunchy in Mike's closet. Perhaps a late night fondling with one of his male friends as an adolescent. Maybe a prostitute on a fraternity vacation. I could only see his white V-necked Hanes, the yellow sweat stains hidden in the armpits.

"Well damn, what do you know," he said when I told him about Bebe Hicks, still flipping through channels. "Did you bring home any leftovers?"

Allie screamed from her playpen, her voice large and endless, another continent. She terrified me. Mike turned up the TV.

"That's all you have to say?" I asked, handing Allie a bottle, which she didn't want.

"What do you want me say?"

"You could ask me how I feel," I said.

Allie was screaming so violently I thought my head might halve, crack like a nut. Sometimes, when she was really tiny, I was scared I might hurt her, or that she'd hurt me. Grow up into one of those angry children who strangles the family dog or slips into your room one night, presses a blade against your throat. This, I did not tell my therapist.

"Well, how do you feel about it?" Mike asked.

"I don't know," I said.

He threw the remote across the room, stalked to the basement. Allie stopped screaming and began crying to herself quietly. Already, she'd learned how to grieve like an adult.

One Saturday afternoon, late in February, the sun crouching pale orange, trees thin and brown and rippling along the highway, exactly the kind of day I had imagined when I had imagined this scenario, I dropped Allie off at my sister's and drove to Waynesville, Alabama. Waynesville is a postcard for the decaying beauty of the Old South. A small town square with a pillared courthouse at its center. Red brick buildings with false facades, gutted and crumbling. A seed store. A hardware store. A five and dime. Old white houses with wide front porches stretching to the sidewalks. I imagined my father there as a child, riding his bike downtown, playing dice or jacks, avoiding stepping on the cracks of those sidewalks. And later, when he'd discovered women, parking in his father's car behind one of those abandoned buildings, peeling the thin, floral dress off Bebe Hicks's body, her thighs trembling, her plump bottom lip caught under her pearled teeth, him pressing himself into her, collapsing from the intensity of it all, promising the promises lovers share against the hush of a newly familiar body.

Lifton Street was full of tiny white houses with green and white striped awnings, front porches with green metal chairs and rockers, fake grass covering the old floorboards, the kind of houses grandmothers live in. Nothing stood out about 658 Lifton Street, except the lawn was covered in cheap statues of urinating cherubs in various poses, some of them in working order, others filled with cans and cigarette butts.

When I imagined Bebe Hicks, I thought of a redneck version of Edna Pontellier. In college, when reading *The Awakening* for the first time, I desperately wished my mother would transform into Edna. She was already indifferent to her children, so that part would be easy enough. I longed for the day I would go home for summer break to find my mother taking scandalous trips to the gulf, throwing dinner parties for the Intelligentsia, hanging out with bohemian artists of indeterminable sexual preference, my father abandoned to her past as an afterthought, a new, young lover sitting at her sun-kissed feet. But in class when we got to the part where Edna, forced to bend to the will of nature and man, "transcends" her painful existence by walking off into the ocean that is woman that is womb that is creator of goddess Edna, I was reminded too much of my mother, who would do just that, make a quiet scene by sacrificing herself like a martyr to the ocean instead of fighting it out. I argued in my final paper that there is no awakening because Edna Pontellier is dead, the exact opposite of awake. DEAD IS DEAD, I wrote in big block letters. My professor argued hers was only a physical death, a metaphorical death, and for a short amount of time, however brief, Edna truly gets to live, and that short time of living is worth more than any lengthy lifetime of not living, of not being who she *really* is.

Only a man would say something like that.

I gave up bohemian mother fantasies. Until Bebe. With Bebe I just changed the story line a bit. Instead of uppity artists and fancy beaches, I inserted Gulf Shores and line dancing. And instead of drowning herself after leaving her husband, too overwhelmed to face the storm, my fantasy Bebe never realized there was a storm brewing, simply rode off in an old red convertible, a silk scarf eddying, a delicate hand throwing a kiss to the air, and her not bothering to look where it fell.

The door of 658 Lifton Street opened to a tall slender woman with phosphorescent skin, eyes the color of freshly cut grass, lips like cherry tomatoes, dimples carving out cheekbones. She had on a gray silk dress layering around her like mist.

I am not exaggerating.

"Yes?" she said.

"Bebe Hicks?" I asked, although I knew the answer. "I'm Adam Wilson's daughter."

"Oh," she said, not looking surprised, "come in."

Her house had rose and peach scarves thrown over the lamps. I thought of Blanche DuBois, worried about the fire hazard, then mentally slapped myself for being so practical.

Bebe's teeth were very white, the whitest teeth I'd ever seen, hypnotizing white. I was scared I might try to touch them without realizing what I was doing. I tucked my hands into my jacket.

"So," she said, motioning me to a zebra-print chair, silver bracelets clacking as she arranged herself on a gold velvet love seat, its lion feet making her look like she was riding the back of a beast, "what can I do for you?"

I hadn't gotten this far in my imaginative musings. I had no idea what I wanted to know.

"My father, you were married to him?" I asked.

"A lifetime ago," she giggled, smiling those teeth. "A sweet boy. Wrote beautiful songs. Like widowed cowboys crying. Voice closest to George Jones of anyone I've ever heard."

I remember Mike telling me a story about George Jones and Tammy Wynette, their tumultuous relationship. His favorite part is where Tammy steals George's keys to keep him from drinking, and George takes the riding lawn mower to the nearest bar, and even after all that, he and Tammy rumbled in love. Mike laughed, called George a dirty old bastard, never even mentioned how Tammy might have felt, who I pictured as thin and hollow, eaten out by love. I thought their story was one of the saddest I'd ever heard, pitiful really. George a hopeless drunk and Tammy even stupider for putting up with it, their emotion too painful and deliberate to bear.

Mainly I was jealous.

Sitting in front of Bebe Hicks, that kind of love made sense, and when I pictured my stern father's face rubbed raw with sorrow and passion, him spray-painting his hurt on Bebe's house, him singing George Jones in such a way that if Bebe would've just listened to the words, really listened, she would've known what her leaving him would do to him, to me, and couldn't have possibly left, couldn't have possibly not understood.

"Oh God," I said, louder than I meant to, "why'd you leave him?"

"We were teenagers when we met," she said.

"And?" I waited for the rest of the explanation.

"Well, you know how it is," Bebe laughed, reached for a cigarette off the coffee table.

I didn't and said so. I wanted an exact why, a moment when everything turned, when everything became clear.

"Why?" she said, puzzled, the tiny lines of her forehead drawing together. "There were no whys. I saw someone else. I left. But your father thought I'd left him for a man with money." She laughed, waved her hand at her cramped home. "Like anyone has money in this town."

"Do you mind?" she asked, pointing to the stereo. "I have to perform tonight and it helps to get me in the mood."

Pasty Cline's warbling, piercing voice filled the tiny den.

"For Christ's sakes," a voice shot from down the hall. "Will you turn that shit down."

"Don't mind her," Bebe said, flipping her wrist. "Luna's sound sensitive. Screams at the birds too."

Luna?

A smaller, younger version of Bebe slipped into the den in waves of red satin.

"Who are you?" she said, plopping down beside her mother.

"Jill Hilbert," I said. Jill. This enraged me. She got Luna and I got Jill, cursed into mediocrity at birth.

"Oh," she said, resting her head on the back of the love seat. She didn't seem to want further explanation.

"She's my ex-husband's daughter," Bebe offered.

"Which one?" Luna snorted.

I know what you might think. That this trip to Waynesville allowed me to unearth the root of my issues with intimacy, showed me that exchanging one life for another simply gets you another set of troubles, and problems are problems. That maybe I went home to my husband, put my baby down for the night, popped open a bottle of wine, turned on George Jones and asked my husband to dance, listening to the words that my father sang to Bebe Hicks in the haze of love.

I didn't.

I listened to another hour of Bebe talking about my father, his proposal at their senior prom, their marriage in the preacher's house on Main, her in her mother's wedding dress, him in a rented suit, their spot on Miller's Creek where they held each other as teenagers and planned their life together, the roses and poetry he left on her doorstep, his voice mingling with hers when they sang on the square, as penetrating as sex, more so really. And then his rage, his agony when she ran off with the first man of many she would run off with in her life, a man whose last name she could no longer recall. There were pictures of Bebe and my father hugging, his smile wide and giving. She showed me letters covered front and back in scrawled, careless script, letters she wouldn't let me read because they were too personal. And the entire time Luna watched, petulant and painfully beautiful, bored with a familiar story, a story like every love story she'd ever know, a story I never knew existed. Her life, her mother's, a country western song.

I felt cheated.

"Do you think I could come see you perform tonight?" I asked when Bebe finished. I'd decided to go the minute she mentioned she was singing. "I won't get in the way."

"Sure," Bebe said. "Luna will pick you up."

Luna rolled her eyes, *hmmmphed*, but said, "Around nine? I

assume you're at the Heart of Dixie since that's the only place to stay in this shithole."

I called Amanda, asked her if she'd keep Allie for the night. Amanda thinks she likes the idea of children. She made Allie a basket at Easter and a stocking at Christmas and sometimes looks at her whimsically and says, "Maybe I should get me one of those," like some people talk about BBQ grills or steam vacuum cleaners. But when it comes time to feed or change Allie's diaper, Amanda's in the bathroom or making a cup of tea or on the phone. I cut her off before she could say no.

Then I phoned Mike. I called him Honey. He hung up on me.

I stopped at the Texaco and bought toiletries and a case of beer. At the checkout counter there was a box of cassette tapes. I asked the cashier, a young black woman with a string of pearls woven through her pile of hair, if she knew some good country music. She stared at me blankly, cocked her chin. I bought every tape with spangles or a cowboy hat on the cover.

I went across the street and rented a room at the Heart of Dixie and called Bebe to let her know what room I was in. Then I walked over to Gail's, the only clothing store in town, and bought a tight pair of jeans, some black boots, and a gauzy magenta shirt that would show your nipples if you were brave enough to wear it without a bra, an idea I entertained for less than a minute. I painted myself up with more makeup than I'd ever worn, thick black liner, lipstick so glossy I thought my lips would slide off my face.

I started drinking.

Fast.

After going through a six-pack and three country tapes, the music began to sound indescribably profound, naked. I found one song by George Jones, "He Stopped Loving Her Today," which reminded me of my father and Bebe. It's about this guy who told the woman who left him he would love her until the day he died. And he did. All of his friends wondered if she'd come one last time to see him at the funeral. And she did. The chorus goes: *He stopped loving her today. They placed a wreath upon his door. And soon they'll carry him away. He stopped loving her today.* I cried at the part where the woman shows up at the funeral. Rewound it to the beginning and played it again so I could cry some more. The people in the next room banged on the wall and told me to shut up.

When Luna showed up late around ten she said, "Good God, what happened to you?" There were beer cans on the floor. Tapes scattered all over the bed. I tried not to wobble.

Luna wore her blonde hair in a braid that brushed against the back of her jeans, her only makeup light coral lipstick. I felt as garish as I did the night of my senior prom, that horrid purple organza gown.

Luna drove an old pickup, which pleased me immensely. On the way there she reached across me, her smell clean, maybe vanilla, opened the glove compartment, pulled out a silver flask and handed it to me.

"You married?" she said.

"Sort of," I said.

She laughed.

"You ever been married?" I asked.

"Never marry. Then your man's got no reason to win you, no incentive to stay. That was my momma's mistake." She grabbed the flask from me, took a pull, handed it back.

"But I thought she was the one who left them?" I said.

"Same difference."

We hit a bump and whiskey sloshed onto my jeans. I didn't try to wipe it up. My thighs vibrated, rippled with the movement of the truck.

"You have kids?" she said.

I thought of Allie. Her constant crying, like a language I almost spoke, could understand if she just slowed down, enunciated.

"No," I said.

We pulled in front of the Moon Wink Saloon, a gray wooden building with beer signs covering the windows. The gravel parking lot, the size of a baseball diamond, was almost empty. We parked up front. A few men in cowboy hats smoked cigars in the entrance, kicked the ground when someone made a joke, spraying dust into the night.

Luna sighed. Grabbed the flask from me. Stared at the bar.

"I have to get the hell out of this town before I kill myself," she said. Then she laughed sharp and high and clipped, put the flask back in the glove compartment, slammed it shut, and said, "Let's go."

The Moon Wink: Thickened women in outdated clothing drinking beers straight out of the bottle. Too-thin men in work shirts the same color as their jeans, skinny lips tugging on cigarettes. Everyone over thirty with skin a wrinkled, freckled, reddish brown. Peanut shells scattered on the floor. Pool balls cracking against each other. The place reeked of liquor and smoke and sweat and bodies, but somehow smelled fertile and rich, like dirt after a rain.

Bebe waved at us, already singing, low and forlorn. She glowed on stage, long and fragile in a low-cut black dress from the seventies, skin transparent, like handblown glass. She was singing a maudlin song I recognized, a song Elvis sings, a song like weeping. *Well hello there, my it's been a long, long time. How am doing? Well I guess I'm doing fine.*

This is what I thought: People get drunk so everything blurs at the edges and the touch of another human being doesn't pierce, and if it does, the hurt's bearable. Until good enough is, well, good enough.

It seemed like a profound revelation at the time. I ordered us another round.

In less than an hour I had to go to the bathroom where I accidentally peed down my legs, pulled my jeans up anyway, put on some more lipstick, and lurched back toward the tables. When I reached our table there was a man sitting across from Luna. I plopped down next to him, introduced myself. He ignored me.

He was young. Late twenties. Almost handsome. Very drunk. He looked like he might cry, kept chanting *fuck, fuck, fuck* and snaking fingers through his hair until his temples stretched taut.

"Luna," he said, "I just don't understand your reasoning." He leaned on the table, tipped my drink over. Ice cubes scattered to the floor.

"Since when do I have to explain my reasoning?" Luna said, handing me her cocktail napkin. Her voice sounded bored.

I leaned back in my chair. Closed my eyes so I didn't have to see the hurt on the man's face. I thought of Allie. Perhaps sleeping, silent for once. Her lids rippling. The smell of her: baby powder, the faint hint of urine. And Mike. One hand on the remote, another across his soft middle. I wondered if he ever tried to imagine what I was doing when away from him, how I looked in his mind's eye.

Luna flicked my cheek, hard. "You passing out on me?" she said. The man was gone.

Bebe was singing the same Patsy Cline song she played earlier in the afternoon. Men stared at her lips, entranced, their hands loose on their beers.

Luna rested her chin in her hand, watched her mother, watched the men watching her.

"She's good, isn't she?" Luna said.

"Wonderful," I said.

"Just something else," she said, downing her drink, then standing up, the table almost flipping over. She nodded her head at the entrance, her braid swinging down her back. "If it's okay with you, I've got to get out of here."

In the truck Luna took the flask from the glove compartment, unscrewed the top, looked at it, screwed the top back on, then threw it out the window past my head. It skidded across the gravel, lodged under someone's tire.

"Good shot," Luna said, laughing. She started the truck. "You cry like that all the time?" she asked, waiting for the engine to warm up.

"What?"

"Inside. With your eyes closed. You were crying."

"I didn't notice," I said, and she touched my knee just long enough for me to know it wasn't accidental.

We turned onto a back road out of the parking lot, gravel spraying. It was February, but the night was unseasonably warm, and the breeze felt good on my face, lessened the blur of the liquor. I settled back into the seat.

"That man in the bar," Luna said after a few minutes, "he asked me to marry him last week."

"Why'd you say no?" I assumed she had from the look on his face.

"Because he's a spinner at the factory," she said, waving a hand at the shacks alongside the road, gray and splintered, almost swallowed by trees and dark, "and this is what love amounts to in my town."

"You never know," I said.

"Yeah," she said. "Yeah, you do."

I closed my eyes. Listened to the night, to the road under the truck, to Luna breathing.

"My father," she said, breaking the silence, "I have no idea who he is. My mother knows, but she says he's not important."

I thought of my father all those years, a cigar in one hand, a scotch in the other, a shadow in his study, classical music playing low, him lost in the vastness of music and emotions without words.

"I don't know my father either," I said. "Not really."

Luna gave no warning.

She shifted gears, slammed her foot against the accelerator. The wind cut sharp against my face. The old pickup shook, the windows rattling inside the doors. Luna's braid whipped against her shoulder. Trees spun past us in blurred shadows, the sky torn with streaks of stars, the cab of the truck thick with gravel and dust. I felt the road give us up.

I put my hands out against the night in front of me, their bones feeble and useless, their flesh pitifully slight. "Luna," I said, in the same manner I reprimanded Allie when she reached for a hot plate or a sharp object, "Stop."

Luna slammed on the brakes. The truck spun off the road, lurched into the woods, pine branches scraping my cheeks, my eyes. The smell of their branches snapping, their needles severing, as pungent as fresh blood. And then we simply stopped.

We sat in silence. Felt our lungs fill with air. Felt our bodies release it.

"I'm sorry, " Luna said after a few moments. Her cheeks were scraped raw, her hair covered in pine needles and branches. She stared straight ahead. "Sometimes," she whispered, "sometimes it's just too much."

I had an affair once, almost. A few years after Mike and I were married. Before Allie.

I was still working, an administrative assistant at a marketing company, although I'd studied literature in college. I handpicked my lover, a coworker from the office, because he was the exact opposite of Mike. A young graphic design artist. Tall. Wiry. Chin-length blond hair, the ends dyed black like they'd been dipped in paint. He talked about the dynamics of yearning and the politics of aesthetics, and after the numbing, repetitive *thud, thud, thud* of my suburban days, he might as well have been popping strawberries in my mouth and whispering in French against my breasts.

We went to a local Holiday Inn. I parked in the back, made him park in the front. The room smelled of Lysol and chlorine and wet towels. He kissed me as soon as the door closed behind us, his breath sweet like peppermints. He said *Darling*. He said *Baby*. He took mouthfuls of me. He took handfuls of me.

But when it came time for us to undress, he stood away from me, carefully unbuttoned his shirt, hung it on a hanger in the closet, then pulled his pants off by the cuffs, matched the creases, shook out the wrinkles and folded them over a chair.

Every movement controlled.

I told him I had to go to the bathroom. Thirty minutes later, he knocked softly, asked me if I was okay. I climbed into the tub. Pulled the shower curtain around me. An hour later he rapped his knuckles hard against the thin door, asked me what kind of game I was playing. I told him I had started my period. He said he didn't care, that it didn't bother him. After another half hour I heard the door to the hotel room click open, click closed.

I dressed. Put on fresh makeup. Stopped at the grocery. I went home and made my husband grilled chicken and asparagus. We watched a talk show on our bedroom TV until he fell asleep, one hand thrown over my belly.

There will be a night.

A night about five years after the night I spent with Luna, when I don't hide in the bathroom. A night I go for drinks with Amanda, who has just divorced husband number five. I will drink too many whiskey sours on purpose. She will nudge my thigh when a young professional walks by, a tall man with a wicked smile full of attitude, and tell me I should say hello, live a little. I will walk with him hand in hand through the parking lot, the night cooler than the night I spent with Luna, although that night will be with me, and I will sober up, notice that the man is slurring drunk, that he's not as good-looking as I thought.

I will go with him anyway.

And afterward, a fuzzy, satin-trimmed hotel blanket pulled to my chin, his presence nothing more than a cooling indentation on the bed beside me, I will think of my sister as a teenager, her nylons torn, her bra hanging from her purse. I will think of my mother frolicking in the pool, her breasts buoyant. I will think of Luna, her hand sweeping against the night with a *This is what love amounts to.* I will think of Bebe Hicks, of her saying, *There were no whys. I saw someone else. I left.*

Only I won't.

I will wash between my legs with hotel soap. I will put on fresh lipstick. Make sure my clothes are tucked in, free of the smell of him. I will go home.

And when I get there, Mike won't ask me where I've been, and I won't tell him. I'll wait until Allie, a sweet, quiet girl in second grade, goes to bed, then tell my husband that I want to go for a ride, that I want to drive. For once, he will agree without asking the wrong questions.

We will drive out of our suburb, past the pale brown stucco squares with two-car garages pushed to the front, some of them open and gaping like wounds. I'll put in an old tape from my glove compartment, one of those I bought the night I saw Bebe Hicks sing, and when "He Stopped Loving Her Today" comes on, I will listen to it as loud as my radio can stand. Rewind it. Listen to it again. When Mike reaches for the volume to turn it down, my look will stop him in midmotion.

When we get far enough out of town that the world isn't covered in concrete or flooded with fluorescent lights, far enough that the night seems alive like we should be, I will pull off onto a gravel road. After a half mile or so, Mike, nervous, shifting, will ask where we are going, and I will ignore him.

The second time he asks, as I know he will, I will be scared, feel the blood thudding through my chest, through my limbs, so fast, so startling, I forget to breathe. But I will remember to punch the gas pedal. I will remember to feel the earth lose hold of us. And I will keep my foot there, firm against the accelerator, and wait for

Mike's gasp of surprise, wait for him to look at me for an explanation, wait for him to hold his own feeble hands out against the world, the ocean of black and stars hurtling toward us, wait for that movement, wait for him to finally understand, to know the word *Stop.*

Some
Things
Collide

———
████████

       Nadine wonders if her recent need to place her hands over the burners on the stove (always counterclockwise in direction), or her insistence on drinking bottled water only (two brands, researched), or her new obsession with fingering a particular lump behind her ear she found at twelve, a discovery which ruined her best friend's birthday party (long story), was her body's way of warning her, preparing her.

She wasn't sure what she was being warned of at first. A fire perhaps, electrical, coursing through her sponge-painted walls while she did something mundane, everyday, like her nails, completely unaware. If she were in a movie, the fingernail polish remover would loom insidiously on the screen, flammable, precarious. Maybe tiny organisms careening in tap water, pincers (do they have pincers?) pinching, her mouth, her esophagus, her intestines lanced. Or fleshy things hidden in flesh. Decay. The body's willingness to succumb. Nadine's fear that the lump behind her ear would move, surge down her neck, across her back, perhaps detouring through an arm, the pulse place at a wrist, on to a hand, through each finger, tracing, shooting up from the middle finger, the one she was told is closest to the heart—shooting up, up, up and slamming into that mysterious, pumping organ in her chest. Nadine at work in her cubicle, her hand clawing at her breast, her eyes O's of surprise. Betty, the annoying secretary who sits next to her, peering around the divide, probably in that ghastly floral dress she wears, her face contorting in attempted concern.

In the end, it was less dramatic than that, as it always seems to be in Nadine's life. No fires in her home. No occupied water. The lump behind her ear standing its ground. Just a tiny new lump in her left breast, which had grown there of its own accord, stationary.

After she discovered it, her obsessive urges stopped. At least, the new ones.

"I knew it," she tells Sandra on their lunch break the day after she receives the results from her biopsy. "I'd expected it for a while." She pushes moo goo gai pan around on her plastic plate. "They take it out next week. Lumpectomy."

The term sounds very clumpy, one of those words that sounds like what it means. She says it again, enunciates. Lump-ect-o-my. She drags out the last syllable, says *me, me, me* several times. The pudgy, Baptist-looking women lunching at the next table begin to stare.

Sandra takes a bite of rice and opens her mouth at the women, lets the rice fall down her chin. The women look at her like she's crazy, then turn away, indignant. Bored women. Boring women. They make Nadine irrationally angry. She has fantasies. There are guns involved. Unresolved anger, she's been told.

"Bitches," Sandra says, rolling her eyes. Sandra resolves her anger right on the spot. She's always like that, ready to jump into a fight. Nadine suspects Sandra was a bully in high school, one of those almost-attractive, big-boned girls who enjoys the social prestige of being the most popular of the unpopular, the ringleader of the rejected. If they had known each other in high school, Sandra would have embarrassed Nadine. Farmer features. Big teeth. Thick limbs. Huge tits. Foul mouth. Nadine played piano at her church and she was the kind of girl who felt it.

Things change.

Sandra and Nadine met at the office ten years ago, both fresh out of Central Alabama Community College. (The students call it CACC, pronounced *kak*, which sounds like something you cough up, a fitting visual for the kind of graduates it produces, or so goes the joke.) Catalogue Creations, where they work, specializes in food-service catalogs. Sandra works in accounting. Payroll. Accounts receivable. Nadine is a desktop publisher. She makes skinny-spined magazines for chain restaurants like Long John Silver's and Taco Bell and Wendy's. Designs layouts and writes copy about ramekins and soap dispensers and deep fryers. Last year she won an award for a Fourth of July sale brochure she did for Sysco's Food Services. She picked a mountain scene, an eagle flying over a snowy peak, and used a red so true that the Sysco emblem looked like a wound in the sky. On the expanse of the eagle's wings she inserted the copy *Sysco's a Soaring Success*, which she'd thought very clever at the time. The inside was all about blenders.

"Look," Sandra says, still pissy about the women at the next table, "I'm sure that it's just a little. Just a spot. They'll clean you out and you'll be on your way."

"A *little* cancer," Nadine says. "Isn't that a bit of an oxymoron?"

"A what?"

Nadine thinks Sandra knows what the word means but is in one of her moods.

"No, seriously," Sandra says. "I'm sure it's nothing much. Probably really localized or they wouldn't have chosen a lumpectomy in the first place."

"They sometimes open you up," Nadine says, "and it's so bad, so far gone, they've got to go ahead and take the whole thing." Nadine still holds on to the childish belief that if you acknowledge something bad might happen to you, if you voice it, then there's less chance that it will. Although, the whole process is tricky because if you consciously try to think of bad things that might happen to you so they won't, then you've negated everything and are right back where you started. It's like doing a good deed and then telling someone about it. You remove the humility. She hasn't figured out a loophole.

"Well," Sandra says, and not unkindly, "then you'll have a mastectomy and we'll get you a new one. The rest of the world buys them, why not you?"

After the doctor gave Nadine the news, she went to the bathroom, took off her shirt and bra, pressed her left breast as flat as she could, pressed until she hurt, and imagined her breast just not existing, at least not on her body, but rather decomposing in a trash bin somewhere like the bad parts of a cut of meat.

"*Ductal carcinoma in situ*," the doctor had said. "Your milk ducts if we're lucky."

Milk ducts. Like a farm animal.

"Should I moo like a cow?" she said, laughing in short bursts.

"Excuse me?" he said, not amused. His nose was long and thin, hooked on the end like a crochet needle.

"Sometimes it's like a fern. Expanding though the milk ducts. A frond, if you will. But localized. Not in the nodes. That's what *in situ* means, 'in place,' " he explained.

In place. Localized. It disappointed her for a flash of a moment, the probable stagnancy.

"A trip!" Sandra says, finishing the last of her sesame chicken, gelatinous and fried, too orange to be edible. "That's what you need to get your mind off things. The beach. Saltwater. It's Memorial Day. We have a long weekend. What do you say?"

Nadine's fortune cookie reads *You are a solitary flower in a field of mediation.*

Nadine wanted to go somewhere quiet, but Sandra pushed for Panama City Beach specifically for its vulgarity. Adventure Islands towering over the strip, full of tacky coffee cups and rock candy and plaques that talk about the difference between being a father and a daddy. Teenagers in shell anklets and shark-tooth necklaces and wraparound shades with greenish blue insect lenses.

Spray-painted car tags in the colors of sunset on big-wheeled trucks with hairless-chested boys who howl at any crease of flesh. A good place to lose yourself. A place where anything goes.

They decide to take Sandra's Miata convertible, which she got in the divorce, because Nadine has a ten-year-old shit-brown station wagon with catsup stains on the seats, a car she's had so long she feels it would be a betrayal to get another, a car that does not fit with their top-down, hair-in-the-breeze vacation.

"I want to do this," Sandra says when she picks Nadine up, handing her a brochure about Panama City. The brochure has a picture of a young woman, a girl really, in a yellow bikini, if you can call it that. Three triangles of fabric and a length of string cutting between her butt cheeks. She's tilting her head back, her wet hair streaming toward white sand in waves reminiscent of the ocean behind her, and she's pouring water over her fake breasts from a conch shell with the same silly, orgasmic expression of lovers drinking from stiletto heels in B-films.

"Only I want to wear a Santa hat and use it for Howard's Christmas card. It'll be funny, a bikini on the beach for Christmas."

Sandra nods toward the backseat, and sure enough, there's a velvet Santa hat sitting on top of an Igloo cooler. Nadine thinks it's jumping the gun, even a little desperate, to be worrying about this six months before the fact, but Sandra's been really vulnerable since the divorce, and looks pained and betrayed when Nadine points it out, although she wears her heart on her sleeve and it's sometimes hard to watch.

"Howard's into quirky photos," Sandra says. "You know, costumes and such."

Howard is Sandra's new boyfriend from Human Resources. Nadine doesn't like him. He wears pastel shirts and Disney ties. Mickey Mouse singing. Daffy Duck playing golf. He breathes heavy, disturbingly so, and has a hint of breasts if you look closely. Nadine can do nothing but. The idea of him dressed in some type of costume, a pirate's patch for example, makes her queasy. Her friend's bad taste upsets her.

"Men are strange," Nadine says. She knows this to be a sage truth.

Nadine once dated an artist from the nearby university. She was in her early twenties and going through her first adult period of discontent. Regression seemed like a good solution. Tom painted death pictures (ugly things made beautiful), played guitar with his teeth (poorly, but they *were* his teeth), pierced his own nipple (why?), and explained in detail how meat rotted in her gut every time she had a hamburger. The typical. One evening she brought body paints over to his place for a surprise. She'd spent a lot of time plotting the wild, mind-numbing sex they were going to have. Props. Positions. Sounds. Declarations. But the night ended with him screaming at her to be still, that she was messing up his work, that her pubic hair made the paint clot.

Clot? This is not a word that sounds appealing in relation to the naked body.

Nadine spent the remainder of the evening sitting on the roof outside his bedroom window, smeared in primary colors, drinking mimosas, one after the other, thinking, I'm butt-naked and obscene, thinking, God somebody notice me and do something, anything. No one did. In the wee hours of the morning her lover poked his head out the window, sighed deeply, shook his head. "You don't understand my passion," he said. Then he went to sleep. Nadine sat on the roof till sunrise, at first trying to rage, then trying to weep, and finally settling on getting drunk and staring into a night and a future that she knew wouldn't include artists or body paints or mimosas on a roof of a crumbling building in the student ghetto. Somehow it was nice, knowing. A relief.

But *cancer?* She certainly didn't see that, either.

"It's just for laughs, " Sandra says, defensively. Nadine can tell she wants for her to say it's okay, normal.

After Sandra divorced a little over a year ago, she went on a whirlwind dating streak, e-mailing the disturbing details of her dates to Nadine every morning. *We did it in the restaurant bathroom.* Or, *An ice cube. Can you believe it?* Nadine, who has never married, thought she'd at least be divorced by now. Maybe even have a kid, the face of whom she pictures in a very watery, hazy kind of way. Her mother sends her books on conquering shyness, where to meet eligible men. Reminds her to wear lipstick when she goes to the grocery store, which Nadine says is silly, but does anyway, always feeling deviant mauling produce in her waxy, red lips.

"I dressed like a nun last week," Sandra says, winking. She plucks a cigarette from a squished pack on her dashboard, jams it between thick lips, and uses a knee to steady the steering wheel so she can work the lighter. The car veers into the oncoming traffic's lane, and even though no one is coming, Nadine fights the urge to steady the wheel.

"A nun?" Nadine says, nose crinkled. Nadine isn't a religious woman. Not anymore. But she likes to keep it as a viable option. Especially the way things are going. It couldn't hurt to look a little pious. Although, Nadine reasons, if there is a God, he would know her protest to be halfhearted, so that might be even worse. How does that go? Either hot or cold? Never lukewarm.

Mainly, it irritates her that Sandra, who isn't very attractive, always has a man, even if they are men like Howard from Human Resources.

"You're such a prude," Sandra says, laughing, which means things are okay between them. When she laughs little clouds of smoke shoot from her wide mouth.

Sometimes, the way Sandra's face moves makes Nadine nervous. She has broad, slack features that expand and contract with alarming elasticity. In fact, everything about her is loose, relaxed. Her eyes slope into her cheeks. Her blonde hair falls long and spare against her chin.

And when she drinks.

Things get really loose, sloppy. Inevitably she starts ranting about her ex-husband, how she walked in on him with a teenage girl from their neighborhood, how the girl called her Mrs. Fincher, which seemed ironic, how she was finally pregnant with his baby, a baby he'd been wanting since they first got married, and how she'd had an abortion the next week and sent a gory pamphlet to his office from one of those pro-life groups on terminating pregnancies, an act that truly scares Nadine, although she tries to be understanding. Sandra finishes by saying that she still sometimes hears her unborn child whispering *why?* It always amazes her, the way people listen to Sandra, the way they call her honey, the way she can cut into herself, open herself up, extract pain, put it on the table in front of her and toast to it. The next day at work, nothing. Just half-moons under her eyes. A sour smell: love gone bad.

Nadine turns up the radio so she doesn't have to talk, flipping through the stations until it lands on a popular song she sometimes hears in stores in the mall. Sandra squeals. Says it's one of her favorites. Booty. Sex. Shake. Booty. Girl. Girl. Booty. Nadine's heartbeat synchronizes with the rhythm of the bass, a startled, erratic pulsing. Sandra sings along in her tinny voice, likes she's been challenged not to miss a word.

Nadine leans back, lets the wind roll over her, watches the clouds mate, mingle, form lions' heads, dragons' flames, a poodle, and for an instant, a young girl in a backbend, her white hair writhing around her like Medusa's.

It's only May, but already the day hovers hot, humid. Nadine can smell herself. She wonders if her scent has changed, if the cancer has altered her body chemistry. She's seen people talk about pheromones and scents on educational shows, the fact that men and women often scout out good gene matches by smell. What if her scent advertises: WARNING, DEFECT. THIS ONE'S A DUD.

She falls asleep with her biceps pulled to her chest, her smell trapped against her, and she doesn't wake until they are pulling up to the hotel, the windshield full of dizzying blue sky, the hotel rising against it, pink, like the meat of a watermelon, spindly palms shooting from patches of grass. The asphalt steams black. A miserable-looking group of elderly women dressed in the colors of sherbet pace in front of a tour bus. A couple argues over how to unpack the trunk while their two kids shriek. A fifties-style sign hangs next to the lobby: The Oasis.

The hotel room is small, decorated in blue, tiny seashells on the wallpaper, a lobster-shaped ashtray. It smells of chlorine and saltwater and bleach, the bathroom faintly of piss, like summer camp commodes. Nadine puts her bags on the bed closest to the door. She wants to take a nap, maybe watch TV. Right now she's usually watching *America's Most Wanted* reruns. Eating pasta. Thinking she should take a run while there is still light. Eating ice cream instead. She can hear splashing and squealing from the hotel pool, the humming of ice machines down the hall, the dull thumping remnants of the dance song from the ride down.

Sandra suggests that they change into their swimsuits and head for the beach bar. She emerges from the bathroom in a neon orange and green leopard-print bikini, her breasts bulging over the top, a sea of fat, liver-shaped sun freckles. Nadine puts on a black one-piece and a sarong with a monkey and parrot print, her white knees poking from the folds, blanched.

They walk to the hotel bar, a thatched-roof, tiki-style set-up, Nadine's flip-flopped feet clicking in a depressed beat behind Sandra's. The bar is full of college kids. Girls with overly tanned bellies and flanks, their hair stringy from the saltwater. Boys with burnt noses, dark chests hairless. Lots of dainty tattoos of butterflies and infinity signs on girls, death-faced skulls and rebel flags on the shoulder blades of boys. Nadine is the only woman in a one-piece. The bartender looks like a bartender. He smiles at them. Calls them ladies in that laid-back bartender way. Sandra orders a girly drink, pinks and peaches, a jaunty umbrella careening off the top. Nadine gets a glass of red wine. Both of them stare into their drinks. The silence between them is louder than the ocean's broil.

Since everyone found out about the lump in her breast—a lump she somehow knew would be there that morning a month ago when she woke to her alarm clock thinking, oh God, another day of deep fryers, thinking, should I drink decaf or caffeinated?, thinking, if I don't wash my hair I'll have time to stop and get gas, thinking all of this and none of this while lifting her arm over her head and massaging her left breast until a tiny, BB-sized lump rolled under her finger—no one has anything to say to her, or if they do, they're scared to say it, scared to talk about their clients or fat thighs or kids' report cards or in-laws or recipes or spouses with her sitting right in front of them, rotting from the inside out. And Nadine doesn't know how to make them feel better, can't remember what she'd ever talked about before.

Food-service items.

She picks up the pretzel bowl off the bar, her fingers nervous, and flips it over to see the manufacturer. Ever since she started working at Catalogue Creations, she searches for the manufacturer's mark on all tableware. If on a date, which doesn't occur often, she has to remind herself to look only when he goes to the bathroom, and if he doesn't go the entire night, it drives her insane, distracts her. She has an almost perfect accuracy rate in guessing the correct manufacturer.

"Libby," Nadine says. She flips the bowl over. Sure enough. "I did a catalogue for them last week. The one with the beer stein on the front."

"Good work," Sandra says, lighting a cigarette. "You know, you're the best at the office."

It doesn't sound like much of a compliment. Nadine tries to be creative, tries to talk customers into four-color catalogs and edgy brochures. Ramekins. They're selling ramekins. Two-inch diameter. Four-inch diameter. Ribbed. Smooth. White. Cream. Not artwork. Not poetry.

She picks up the ashtray. Guesses Continental. Looks for the logo. Right again.

"Let's leave work at work, " Sandra says, grabbing the ashtray and snubbing her cigarette out in a way that lets Nadine know she's irritated or bored.

Nadine bites her lip. Draws the clouds she saw earlier in the sand with her big toe. Sandra orders another round. Lights another cigarette. There's a sand dune restoration project all along the beach, ugly orange tape warning tourists to keep off, picket fences huddling around pitiful mounds of sand. Nadine feels a kinship to the sand dunes—she's shifting, settling, critically eroding. There's a project under way to restore her.

She keeps this to herself, her grand metaphors. This is a new affliction, symptomatic.

"Give me one of those," she says, pointing to Sandra's Virginia Slims.

"You don't smoke," Sandra says.

"I already have cancer," Nadine says. "What can it hurt now?"

"You shouldn't talk like that," Sandra snaps. "It's weird."

Nadine answers by taking a cigarette and lighting it. Her tongue, her throat burns. She imagines the smoke filling her lungs, thick and scorching. Only in her mind her lungs don't look like human lungs, but rather like fish gills, the bass of her childhood camp days, her bare foot against a scaled belly, a hook tugging the corner of the mouth taut, the gills feathered and red and frothing against the pier.

Surly.

It makes her happy, pissing off her body. Right now, she'd smoke two at a time if she could.

"You know," Sandra says, "we all just want to help you. You have to let us, though, you understand?" Sandra looks very earnest, like she's been working up the courage to say what she'd just said for a while now.

Nadine has no idea who this "we" is. Betty, the secretary? Do she and Sandra talk about her by the coffee machine in the morning? Say things like, *It makes you realize how short life is. All we can do is be there for her.* Or maybe the "we" is Sandra and Howard. Maybe they talk about her breast cancer in that quiet moment after love making, Sandra's nun or French maid costume in a puddle on the floor, Howard cupping Sandra's own large breast, Sandra saying *Could you imagine how awful it would be to be sick and all alone?*, the moment sweeter because they realize how close death could kiss, thankful that it had missed them this time.

"I was watching one of those investigative reporting shows," Nadine says. "About bank robbers. And there's this one famous bank robber who stole a million bucks, and when they finally caught up with him a year or so after he'd committed the robbery, they found him penniless. When asked how in the world he could have wasted a million dollars in a year, he replied, 'Half of it I spent on gambling, booze, and women. The other half I squandered.'"

She was sixteen. That day in the backyard of Mill Merrills's house, him slim-hipped and swaggering. Lighting the wrong end of the cigarette, nervous in trying to impress her. Her saying, *Gross, Mill Merrill,* in the affected voice of her mother, her voice now. Somehow, the decision not to be *that* kind of girl, the kind who would sneak cigarettes in the dusk with a neighborhood boy, felt like a turning point in her life, began defining the kind of girl she would be, the kind of woman who assumed she didn't have any life to squander, the kind who didn't get any extra.

"He lived big," Nadine explains. "He knew he was going down, and he lived big. You see what I'm saying?"

Sandra looks dazed, out of the loop. Nadine has no idea what she's saying either. The wine and the nicotine make her head spin. She puts her cigarette out.

More silence.

A squeal cuts through the afternoon, opens in Nadine's belly, sharp. A group of teenagers are wrestling in the hotel pool. Three boys, all lean and brown, sleek creatures, their too-long hair singeing the napes of their necks, wrists and ankles circled in cheap, souvenir jewelry. Two girls, maybe eighteen years old, both in racy bikinis, the kind you have to sneak out of the house with. One of them is beautiful, tall and slender, defiant in a pair of blood-red cat sunglasses, already painfully aware that everyone is aware of her. The other girl is less attractive, short and curvy, a body that promises spread and soon. The less attractive girl is the one who squealed, probably to compensate for the fact she is less attractive, already painfully aware that everyone else is aware of her friend. The boys are chasing the girls around the pool, threatening to throw them in, and the girls pretend to put up a fight, although they allow themselves to be caught and then make a big affair of climbing up the ladder out of the pool, arching backs and running fingers thought wet hair in a Playboy pose. A few of the elderly women from the tour bus are hunkered down in lounge chairs on the other end of the pool, their clumpy flesh pushing through the slats of the chairs. They watch the kids disapprovingly. Cluck tongues and shift gams.

"Party time," Sandra screams, lifting her drink in a toast to the kids.

The boys toast back halfheartedly, and the less attractive girl rolls her eyes. The pretty one doesn't even bother.

"Bitches," Sandra says as loud as she can without yelling.

Young, Nadine thinks, that's what they are. Pretty. Unbroken. Knowing hasn't come upon them, a thief in the night. Nadine works to avoid blurting out an even worse metaphor.

Sandra's yells catch the attention of two men sitting at the bar. They're in their mid-twenties, both in golf shirts and nylon swimming trunks and fading purple and yellow Mardi Gras beads. The blond one with the mullet saddles up next to Sandra, wraps an arm around the back of her chair, offers to buy her a drink. The redhead has a gap between his front teeth that flashes pink with tongue when he smiles, which he won't stop doing at Nadine.

The men ask the questions men ask women at a bar. They laugh deeply. They gesticulate. They hold in their beer guts.

Sandra answers with answers women offer to men at a bar. She giggles. She tosses her hair. She crosses her legs in the manner that makes her thighs look the thinnest.

Nadine stares sullenly at the ocean, trying her best to ignore the redhead, who by now she knows is named Chet.

"It's amazing, isn't it?" Chet says. He's one of the palest people Nadine has ever seen, watery pale, like breast milk. Nadine remembers what Hattie, the black lady who helped her mother out now and again, used to say about white people. She said they were living ghosts, said they smelled dead, which inspired Nadine to douse herself in her mother's expensive French perfume and earned her a severe spanking. Chet smells like vodka and sweat.

"I mean it's so grand," Chet continues. "So massive. Perpetual."

"I guess," Nadine says, still not looking his way. "If you get into that sort of thing."

The sun is just beginning to set, and the ocean blazes red, orange, green. Chet's cheesy come-on reminds Nadine of a guy she met at party once who tried to pick her up by pointing to the moon and telling her how at that moment she was touching everyone and everything in the universe, including the moon, something about molecules touching molecules touching molecules. Nadine laughed in his face at the time, but she never forgot it.

"Look," she says, finally turning toward Chet, "are you really going to bother?"

"I guess not," he says. He seems almost relieved, and they sit in silence, both staring into the ocean.

Perpetual?

When Nadine was eleven her Great Aunt Ruby came to her house to die. She brought three parakeets, two cats and an aquarium full of exotic fish with long, elegant tails that unfurled around their sleek bodies in a hypnotic dance. Aunt Ruby loved her birds and cats, but fussed over those fish with the passion of a new mother. She stood in front of the aquarium for as long as she could stand. She clucked. She cooed. She clapped. And on bad days, when she couldn't get out of bed, she made Nadine prop her up with pillows until she could see the aquarium on the dresser, the fish unnaturally beautiful, their bodies slicing through silence.

By the time she arrived at Nadine's house, Aunt Ruby was swollen where she should be slim and sunken where she should be fleshy. She had ovarian cancer, which Nadine knew from listening to her mother talk on the phone, could gnaw you to the quick in a matter of months. Aunt Ruby had a complete hysterectomy in her thirties, but the doctor left a tiny piece inside of her by accident.

"Ours is not to question," Aunt Ruby would say, but Nadine did and felt guilty for it.

"So one day, I just won't *be?*" she'd ask her aunt over and over again. This seemed impossible, made her mind skip.

"Don't be silly," Aunt Ruby said. "The soul is perpetual."

The day Aunt Ruby died, Nadine found all of her fish laid out on a doily on a little silver tray. It was obvious that her aunt arranged them with great love, their fins and tails perfectly flat, like pinned butterflies. Nadine was devastated. She wanted to care for them, to grieve with them, to coo and cluck and clap. That was to be her homage.

That afternoon she looked up *perpetual* in the dictionary. *Eternal, everlasting, constant, continual, as in perpetual damnation.*

"Hey," Sandra says, wedging between Nadine and Chet and linking an arm around each of them. "No somber faces. This is a vacation." She jerks her head toward the blond guy with the mullet. "Alan here is going to take that Santa picture of me while there's still some light. He says he took a photography class in college. You going to be okay while we run to my room and get my camera? Chet'll take good care of you, won't you Chet?"

Nadine shrugs.

Chet nods.

Less than a minute after Sandra and Alan disappear, Chet excuses himself to go the bathroom. Ten minutes later, none of them has returned. Someone turns on a radio. A car salesman looking guy tells Nadine her sarong has a lot of character. A young woman cries by herself at a table in the corner, her sunburned face flushed and puffy, a few rednecks circling her like sharks. Another bartender comes on shift.

Although Nadine sometimes feels like killing herself, she does not want to die. This is what she thinks, and then tries not to think.

When Sandra finally returns from the beach, her Santa hat and camera dangling from her wrist, the first thing she asks is where Chet is, and her tone lets Nadine know that Sandra thinks it's her fault that he's not around.

"He got lost on the way to the bathroom," Nadine says. She laughs at her own joke.

"We'll have to take y'all's car then," Alan says, his thick arm noosed around Sandra's neck, his chin tucked on her shoulder. "Chet's got our keys."

"We want to ride on the strip," Sandra explains. "You know, cruise like in high school." Alan's grinning behind Sandra, his redneck mullet irritating the hell out of Nadine, and him pretending not to see Sandra mouth, "Isn't he hot?", her eyes pleading for Nadine not to mess this up.

"You kids have fun," Nadine says, standing. Her head swims from the wine and her chest feels like a boulder has rolled over it. "I'm going to bed." She's done high school once and it sucked the first time.

Sandra balks and Alan says c'mon and then they're in the car, Alan's hand between Sandra's legs, Nadine driving, which she gets the sense was her purpose from the get-go since Alan and Sandra can barely stand up. They sit at the intersection of the hotel parking lot and the strip for a full ten minutes, staring at the cars inching by, girls sitting on the tops of convertibles, boys stomping in the back of pickups, everything a slow whirl of neon lights and bright swimsuits and glinting teeth.

Finally, a car lets them cut in, and they pull up behind a red Ford pickup so shiny Nadine knows the owner is one of those small-town boys who carries a rag in his back pocket to wipe off fingerprints on the door handle after he opens the door for his girl. The back is full of teenagers beer bonging, at least ten of them, and Nadine cannot discern where one body ends and the next one begins.

Alan takes a pull off a flask he got from somewhere, then hands it to Sandra, who hands it to Nadine, who holds it.

"You know," Alan says while they wait for the cars to start moving, "my mother had her breast taken off and she's doing right well. In fact, she had this tattoo of a goddess and some roses and vines and stuff done over the scar. She says it's her way of getting her body back."

Nadine glares at Sandra, who pretends not to notice.

"It really is kind of pretty," Alan continues. "She let me see it. There's not a breast there anymore so it's not like you're looking at something you shouldn't be looking at on your momma."

"I'm having a lumpectomy," Nadine says. "They're going to cut it out of me. Just the lump. Then give me some radiation for a while." She sees her breast flayed open, the milk ducts plant-looking, as the doctor described, their fronds wrapped around a tumor, ruby colored and smoothed round like a jewel or stone, the design almost ornate. She knows from the pictures the doctors showed her that cancer looks like nothing so natural.

"Yeah, well," Alan says, irritated that she didn't take to his concept of reclaiming the female body, "it's just an idea."

All Nadine can think is that surely a long string of bad decisions, half-baked choices, had led her to where she was at that moment. Sober. Pretending she isn't almost middle-aged. Sitting next to Sandra, a friend who isn't really a friend. Pretending that her pretend friend isn't getting felt up by a redneck wannabe–golf pro dishing out breast cancer recovery suggestions.

It all makes Nadine wish she'd done things differently. Makes her wish. She wishes she'd gone back to school to get a real degree instead of her associate's degree, like her mother suggested five years ago, advice she ignored mainly because it was her mother's advice. She wishes that she'd stuck with her Spanish, that she'd studied instead of watching soap operas or reading fashion magazines, that she could roll her Rs at the drop of a hat. She wishes she'd gone out with the short, angular-faced man with the wicked goatee who had struck up a conversation with her about antioxidants in the Bruno's produce section last year around Christmas. She wishes that she had gone to Paris to live as an exchange student in high school when she had a chance, instead of allowing her boyfriend (who ditched her that very year for an overdeveloped cheerleader) to convince her that he couldn't exist apart from her, that she couldn't exist apart from him.

She'd existed.

Nadine thought of the young girls at the pool, their confidence, their disdain at Sandra, a thirty-two-year-old woman howling like a perpetual teenager. Twice their age and still sitting on a redneck beach strip in Panama City, Florida, in a string of cars back to back and not going anywhere.

Nadine can't seem to escape her bad metaphors.

"Good God, are we going to move or not," Alan says, almost on cue.

The cars in front lurch forward and Nadine looks up at the road just in time to see a girl's body tumbling off the edge of the red pickup, almost gently, hair streaming, like divers off the edge of a boat in a Jacque Cousteau documentary. It takes her a moment to realize that she didn't rear-end the truck, that the truck bumped into the vehicle in front of it. The collision was so slight it should have barely jarred the vehicles, a shudder.

For a moment no one moves. Then the cars behind them start honking. Alan grabs the flask and chucks it out into the street. Sandra whimpers, "Oh God." Nadine waits for the girl to stand up, to offer a graceful bow, to climb long-limbed back into the truck, hands reaching for her, but she doesn't. She lies limp on the asphalt, her body bent awkwardly, her skin shimmering with the neon lights of the strip.

Everyone in the truck starts moving at once, boys jumping over the side, girls poking legs over the tailgate, huddling at the back of the truck. One of the boys hesitantly touches the hurt girl, like a kid poking an animal on the side of the road to see if it moves. When he finally stretches her lengthwise, trying to stabilize her neck, her long hair falls from over her face.

The beautiful girl from the pool. The one with cat-eyed sunglasses.

Only it isn't.

The bone structure is all wrong. This girl has a wide nose and a chin too small for her face. Blood bubbles from her mouth. The wrist of her left hand is bent forward, like those kids with muscle problems.

For a moment Nadine is terrified by her sense of relief, wonders why it is somehow easier for her to watch the suffering of a girl she has never seen before. She thinks of Tom, her artist, all those gory paintings, his long speeches about owning the disparities of life, how ugly things, such as death, could be made beautiful, how perception is constructed by society.

At this moment she wishes she could slice him open, thrust her fist into his belly, then open her palm, her fingers spreading, growing inside him like life or death, but painful all the same.

"It's a good sign that they took her off in the ambulance with the sirens sounding, right?" Sandra says later, as they finally pull into the hotel parking lot. "That means she's alive, doesn't it?"

They're all shocked sober. Alan has the door of the Miata half open, ready to bolt, before Nadine even turns the ignition off. He barely kisses Sandra on the cheek, then skunks off into the night. Nadine and Sandra walk to their room. They take turns washing their faces, brushing their teeth. They put on their nightgowns and climb into their beds, the paper-thin hotel sheets pulled to their chins, the TV flickering on mute, Jay Leno interviewing a supermodel whose name Nadine can't remember.

The ocean rushes the shore. The ceiling fan whirls. The music from the tiki bar rolls through their window. Still, the silence between them is deafening.

"Nadine," Sandra whispers. "Are you awake?"

Nadine answers by turning over.

"I can't sleep," Sandra says, sniffling. "I can't stop thinking about that girl there all crumpled. She was so young. And it shouldn't have hurt her at all. Do you think she'll be okay?"

"I don't know," Nadine says. She doesn't. And for some reason it makes her angry the way Sandra is responding to the tragedy of that girl, the way she tries to own others' sorrow, the way she uses it to remind her how precious her own life is.

"Nadine," Sandra whispers again. "You won't tell anyone in the office about Alan, will you? We were just flirting and I'd hate for Howard to get the wrong idea."

Nadine didn't mention Sandra's unmade, rumpled bed when they arrived back at the hotel, not out of respect or some sense of discretion, but because she knew that Sandra would want to talk about it, to absolve herself, and Nadine has run out of sympathy.

"I know she's okay," Sandra says a few minutes later. "It just wouldn't make sense for that little fall to hurt her too bad." She has stopped crying, has convinced herself of something.

Outside the moon passes behind a veil of clouds. A woman laughs from the pool. A couple argues in the next room. A door slams. The moon reappears, unyielding.

Nadine feels something loosen in her chest, feels her molecules colliding—something growing, expanding, moving outside of her.

Only Ends

When Quinn showed up at our door with Marcy I wouldn't open it even though he rang twice. Momma said, What are you, a nut? Open the damn door. So I did. Marcy was thin like a branch with the same knobby knots on her chest and she smelled of baby powder and some other perfume I didn't like. She had on a blurry shirt made from pink feathers and a pink skirt showing no-color legs. Quinn found her at the university.

Quinn said, Hey kid, which he'd never said before, and fluffed my hair, which he'd never done before neither. I'd spent over an hour in Momma's bathroom rolling my bangs and spraying them and then rolling them some more till the curling iron layered over sticky. Momma kept screaming, Don't burn the house down, Sissy, and I said I ain't, and used her razor to clean off the gook. My friend Samson told me that if you run out of cockroach killer you can use hair spray and it will do the trick. I worried that Momma might knick herself with the hair-sprayed razor and the poison would go to her blood and she'd die, but then I figured she's a lot bigger than a cockroach.

Momma put Marcy in the high-backed yellow silk chair in the living room where we never sit, so everyone shuffled, not knowing which seat was theirs. I took the couch because it had flowers spread wide and I could pretend I was birthing out of one like a cartoon character. Marcy was nervous, you could tell, and kept folding and unfolding her legs and shifting her bones in the chair. So I folded and unfolded my legs and shifted myself about the couch until Marcy looked anywhere but at me and Momma stared straight though me.

Nobody said nothing to me because what would they say?

My momma says that as an almost baby in her belly I stole the life from the other half of me, which, according to my momma, shows my general sour nature. I sucked the food right from my sister's growing body till the little body didn't grow no more, but shriveled like bad fruit and spoiled and my momma's belly ached and her blood boiled poison and the doctors had to gut her like a bass and yank me from her blood-wet. And even after all of that stealing from my sister who never became my sister, I didn't steal enough to grow myself a full brain, which, according to Momma, shows my general lazy nature. They named her Sadie and buried her under a stone with a lamb riding it that says *Sadie Jenkins Life Only Ends on Earth*. On bad days I've walked to see her and talked some and then answered back for her, figuring that if she's my twin she'd say what I'd say, so we talk a lot.

So as not to scream at me, Momma went into the kitchen to get shrimp on creamed cheese crackers and offered them to Marcy, who curled her nose but took one anyway and traded it back and forth between her little hands.

Quinn planned on marrying her the next day.

Momma made me a pink dress like Marcy's pink sweater and

pink skirt, like the other girls who were going to stand in the front of the church not talking and not moving but smiling sweet like ladies and not causing trouble. It had lace on the collar and pearl buttons down the back, and when I said that's stupid, putting them buttons down the back where I can't see them, Momma said they were for others seeing me. I said I thought I was supposed to stand in the front of the church not moving and not talking and not causing trouble and facing the people. Momma said shut up.

Marcy didn't want me in the pink dress. I heard Momma talking to Quinn the week before and Momma said, She's your sister, she has to be in the wedding. I don't know what Quinn said because he was at the university, but Momma said back, She's lost weight, Quinn, we'll tuck her on the end. The other girls have bones in their skin and me only fat. Momma bought me weights and an exercise tape for Christmas last year and I watch it more than I do Disney.

Marcy has a nose like the hook on the bathroom door that my towel slides off of and Momma screams, Sissy, don't leave wet towels on the floor. Because of the perfume and the nose and the pink dress I'd decided I didn't plan on liking her. Marcy's parents don't like her neither, or they don't like Quinn's liking her, or her liking Quinn. Marcy's a Catholic and loves statues of Mary and talks to priests in wooden boxes because Catholics ain't allowed to talk to Jesus straight. And they got a problem with us? Momma said.

I was bored of Marcy and her shuffled shrimp cracker and so I asked to go outside and Momma said fine, and Quinn fluffed my head messing my hair and said, Have fun, kid, which he'd only done once before, and my bangs were hard and pointy against my forehead like the needles Momma sticks in my fat twice a day for my bad blood.

Bad blood. Bad Sissy.

Samson was outside in his front yard looking for ants to blow up. I said, Hey Samson, and he said, Hey retard, but he said it nice, not like the others. Samson's nine. I'm fourteen. We're best friends since Laura Field moved away last summer. She was his best best friend.

On my fourteenth birthday Momma had me a party with the other kids, which were three, and we had a cake with pink icing and white icing and there was a Barbie doll on the top like I asked for but Momma put wings on it to make it an angel and so it was an angel Barbie but everyone still got jealous and I lost the sack race.

Samson said, Shut up about your stupid birthday party. I was there, remember?

I'll be there, my daddy said the week before my birthday. I promise. But he sent a present instead, this hippo that eats balls, and I beat Samson five times till he slammed the hippo flat and footballed the game into the gully behind our house. I didn't cry but Samson did.

I asked Samson could I blow up ants too, though they looked sad scattered around and bent up. Say, Samson said, you ever ate chocolate-covered ants? I said no, so he picked up an ant, and said how about dirt-covered ants? Then he stuck it down my shirt but not in my mouth and his mouth was open and laughing so I laughed too.

HA. HA. HA.

Samson has thick glasses that have more dirt than glass and he's littler than the other little kids. Bigger kids break his glasses, but he has a second pair. They say white trash. Whore for a momma.

Sometimes bruises eat up Samson and his hands ball tight like fists when he's not noticing me noticing him and his father leaves for a while and his momma makes Noodle Roni for breakfast but doesn't eat and smokes instead and it's mine and Samson's favorite breakfast.

You can blow up ants if you let me feel your titties, he said.

I have big ones because I'm fat. Samson grabbed one and squeezed it and said look, I'm milking a cow, milking a cow. Moo like a cow and we'll play farm.

MOO. MOO. MOO.

But we blew up ants instead with Black Cat firecrackers. Stuck'm down in the bottom of the dirt pile, little black ants rolling over white nubby eggs. And I lit one side and Samson lit the other and we ran, but I didn't get as far as Samson, and he screamed, You're going to blow up, you're going to blow up! But I didn't and the ants did and they blew in the air with their legs running, and I felt sorry for them but didn't tell Samson. Just laughed.

HA. HA. HA.

On special days my momma sits on the back porch and shoots off fireworks out of the bottles at her feet. The last Christmas my daddy was here we had smoked turkey and I asked, Does that mean the turkey smokes cigarettes? and no one laughed. My momma was shooting fireworks off in her bathrobe with her titty hanging out and caught the porch on fire and Daddy said, Goddamn, and Momma said, Just leave.

Daddy found God and lives with Him and his new wife Ellen in Wetumpka.

Samson said, I hear your brother's getting hitched up to some fancy girl from the university. He's a big man now. Big engineer man. Going to wire her good.

My brother ain't much bigger than me so that's what I said, and Samson rolled his eyes like he does and told me to give him some bubble gum. I said I ain't got any, and he said, So what's in your mouth? I gave him my last piece though I wanted it myself. I can fit up to eight pieces in my mouth at once and sometimes I do so Sampson can't have none, and Momma slaps me on the back of the head and says spit that mess out. I hide them chewed up like Play-Doh under my bed and pick them off to make shapes like roses when I can't sleep.

When Quinn left for college he said, I ain't coming back, you hear me? But my momma didn't because she was sleeping with her bottles on the couch and he came back next break anyhow. Quinn's sad because of my head, Momma says. Sad because his head ain't like mine, or because mine ain't like his.

Grandma drove up and I tried to hide behind Samson's bushes so I didn't have to go visiting, but Grandma sees everything and said, Get on out of there, you're going to hurt yourself, I'll be back for you in a minute, and then went in my house. My house is peeled yellow like a banana. I'll paint it next spring, Daddy said. Why don't you just leave and live with her, Momma said. You're already gone anyway.

Grandma fell asleep on the beach when she was young and thin and beautiful and had ten boyfriends at once with jobs and fancy cars and drinks with umbrellas in them, and the sun stroked her too hard and she lost her hair and it never grew back, but I'm not supposed to talk about it.

Sometimes Grandma and I find Momma naked and asleep on the toilet with bottles at her feet but no bottle rockets and her fat spills over the seat like toilet water and the hair on her thingy is gray and her titties hang low like died balloons and we have to try to move her to bed. Grandma says, Lord have mercy. Lord have mercy.

Daddy lives with the Him too in Wetumpka with his new wife Ellen.

Grandma came out of the house and said, Let's get going, and I got in her car like a boat but bigger and slower and we drove over to Mrs. Melon's house, who'd been dying for a long time. She sure is a pretty thing, Mrs. Melon said from her bed, and patted my head with her sausage hand and her arm, purpled and sucked up like raisins which I hate but Samson likes. A sweet girl like you! she said like she always said, some boy'll be snapping you up in no time. Just wait and see. Just like my Paul.

Daddy has a new little girl with a whole brain.

Mrs. Melon pointed to Paul, who gave her his name, and shined his picture again like she did the day before and the day before that. Paul's hugging an island tree and looks skinny and scared and has on a war costume.

After we left my grandma said, That woman's crazy loving a man that ain't been a man for over fifty years. Be glad you're not getting married on account of your head, she said. Man don't have enough sense to know where his bread's buttered. Even dogs knows who it is that feeds them. Man carries his sense in his drawers, and when he leaves, your life in his back pocket. Grandma's well-known for saying such as that.

When we got home Marcy was still sitting in the yellow chair, but she'd changed to jeans that hid her bones except her elbows that pointed angry and because of her elbows and her nose and her perfume I didn't like her.

Quinn said, Why don't the two of you go take a walk and get to know one another. Marcy couldn't say no so she didn't, but she talked to me in that voice people use to talk to me. So, she said, what grade are you in now? You're just growing up. Growing up from what? I said since she never saw me grown down. After we walked around Wilkins Drive for a bit, I was still not talking and her trying, and I said, I don't want to take a walk, I want to take a ride and I want to drive. Then I was behind the wheel of Quinn's truck and she said, Are you sure your momma approves? And I said, Oh yeah, I drive all the time. Which was true, because I go to the arcade with Samson on Saturdays sometimes and we play Super Race 2000 and I always lose. But we wouldn't that Saturday because Quinn was marrying Marcy and I added that to the reasons I hated her. I stole the keys out of Quinn's jacket.

I made it out the driveway okay and Samson's daddy knocked down our duck mailbox once anyway and Momma put up another but it's a dog and I didn't hit it so I felt good. Marcy's pink fingers were working. Are you sure this is okay, Sweetie? she said in that voice and I sped up.

When we got to the end of the block, she said I'd better turn around because we hadn't told anyone where we were going, and I said, You're going to let me stand in the front of the church in my itchy pink dress, ain't you? And she said, Of course, you're Quinn's kid sister and we're family almost, and she was smiling that smile people smile at me.

I hit the stop sign and we stopped. Marcy was crying, her hooked nosed bleeding tears and snot and I tried to put my fist through the windshield but the glass stopped it and she got out of the truck running.

Bad. Bad. Bad, my head said banging.

Momma wrapped my hand and head and we ate dinner and didn't talk about it. Roast beef and lemon icebox pie that I'm not supposed to eat on account of my bad blood, but I did when I cleared the table, scraped what was left on their plates off with my finger, then sucked my finger clean like usual, tugging with my tongue and cheeks till my finger ached red.

I heard Marcy say to Quinn, You give that girl too much slack, treat her like a child. She'll be what you make her. Shut up, Marcy, he said. You have no idea what they've done to her. And Marcy stomped into the bathroom and I watched my exercise video imagining myself a branch growing long with knobby breasts and elbows.

Momma pricked my finger and gave me a shot in my fat and I didn't cry and she said, I just don't understand why your sugar's always off. It never ends, does it, Sissy?

Momma says I poisoned her in her belly making them gut her like a bass and yank me out blood-wet, but my therapist said she poisoned me, and how do I feel about that?

Samson showed up later at the window knocking. His cheek

was a bruise instead. You think I can sleep at your place tonight? he said hopping. In your closet or something? And it would have been fun, Samson spending the night, but I said naw because Momma wouldn't let him with Marcy storming in the bathroom and Quinn mad about his truck and so I shut the window and he left small in the dark.

Since Laura Field moved, I'm Samson's best best friend.

We woke up to wedding day and Marcy crying because she'd lost her momma and daddy and lost her parties and lost everything that weddings are about and was going to have a fat girl on her stage. Shut up, Quinn said, she'll hear you. And it wouldn't be proper for us to have the whole shebang considering.

She cried through the entire wedding too, her side of the church almost empty, and I stood quiet and not causing trouble with my pearl buttons down the back no good to nobody because they couldn't see them. Mrs. Melon wheeled in with oxygen and her Paul picture and said more than once how it reminded her of her wedding day while rubbing his glass face. Mrs. Melon died a few weeks later and now Grandma and I visit Mrs. Trinkle down the street. It never ends, does it, Sissy? Grandma says when they put them in the ground.

I'll be coming, Daddy said, I promise. But he sent real silver spoons and forks and knives instead.

We went to my house for the reception and Marcy and the other pink girls who are stringy with huge yellow hair like weed flowers giggled and giggled and moved every time I came close but always smiled me that smile. Marcy cried over the reception even though we put shrimps on everything and bought those fold-out bells at Wal-Mart and I was good and didn't cause trouble.

Momma kept tripping and drinking the punch that stank and wrapping fat arms around Quinn saying my baby my baby my baby. Everyone danced with everyone except me, and I danced alone and chewed four pieces of bubble gum to the music till I got a headache and I climbed under the reception table and stuck it there and it looked like a poodle or a cloud.

Samson was supposed to come for me but his momma called and said he was sick like he is a lot.

It was dark enough that I couldn't remember when it had been light when Momma called everyone in a circle and said she was sending her baby off like old times, and she whipped out some bottle rockets and Quinn clapped and Marcy looked at her white slippers that she said earlier weren't the right shade, and Grandma said, Good God, how many whites are there?

Momma squatted fat on the porch and everyone was yelling and she lit some bottle rockets and aimed them out of her bottle at the sky and *FFSHHHhhh*, like opening a coke bottle. Quinn clapped and said nobody but his crazy momma, and Marcy smiled too, but that nose hooked mean. Momma's mouth was leaking and her lipstick snuck down her chins. She pulled out a thick rocket and said it was the special one and everyone cheered and she held it lit over her head talking about her baby, her baby grown up, and *boom* went her thumb, blooming blood and scattering in pieces like those bent-up ants.

Momma held her thumb that wasn't there no more and said, Why'd he leave me? Why'd he leave me like this? What kind of man leaves a woman to this? No one answered anything but their feet. The night swelled shut like one of Samson's black eyes.

Sometimes I tell Sadie about Momma being sad that Sadie left us, and Sadie never answers that one back, even if I scream and curse and kick the stone with the lamb riding it that says *Sadie Jenkins Life Only Ends on Earth*.

After Grandma took Momma to the hospital everyone went home, and Quinn and Marcy packed up their things and she said she's never, never in her life, Oh God, what a horrid beginning. Quinn told her to shut up. On their way out he fluffed my hair like he does and said, Take care, kid, and then they drove off with the stop sign dent till their taillights smudged into black and then nothing.

I sat on the front steps waiting for the night to end or open up like Samson's fist when he sees it's a fist or Momma's laugh when it's not poisoned or Sadie's voice growing wide in my head when she speaks, or maybe even with magic, like one of those cartoon flowers blooming and unfolding in a matter of seconds, and the cartoon birds chirping and the animals with voices singing and the sun new and coppery, like it'd just been drawn and colored fresh.

What
Kind
of
Man

———
█████████

      Elsie didn't realize she'd been staring at Jimmy long enough for her coffee, the cup clenched between both hands, to go cold. He was mowing the grass, his tropical shirt so damp the white flowers smeared pink with flesh. Limp hair swept over his crown. Occasionally he'd pass by the window, see her standing there, wave.

      When she woke earlier that morning and leaned over to nudge him, his space in their bed was empty, his pillow covered in hair. She picked up a strand and held it to the morning light. Infused with sun it looked almost radioactive, as if its DNA had been spliced with that of a jellyfish, which seemed commonplace these days. She twirled it for a moment, ran it over her closed eyelids, tickled the insides of her nostrils, then flicked it away.

So he wouldn't be upset, Elsie removed the pillowcase from his pillow, took it to the bathroom, and shook it in sharp *cracks* until the hair sifted with the dust into the tub. She turned on the shower and watched it disappear.

As a girl, when Elsie took the *What-Kind-of-Man-Is-Your-Man?* quizzes, or made lists with her girlfriends about where she would live and how tall her husband would be, or changed her surname in loopy script in school notebooks, or pictured what her husband-to-be was doing at that very moment, breathless that he existed out there somewhere, waiting for her, she never once imagined she'd be married to a bald man.

Who does?

With Felix yipping at her feet for breakfast, she shuffled to the kitchen with the intention of making coffee and pancakes, only to find freshly brewed coffee waiting for her, and pancakes, doughy in the middle and burned on the edges, soggy in syrup, sitting on the kitchen bar. Spilled batter had coagulated along the table and across the burners. It took her the better part of ten minutes to scrape it from the ridges of the stove with a toothpick. She made herself a cup of coffee, dumped the pancakes in Felix's dish, and leaned against the kitchen window to watch Jimmy mow grass.

It was six o'clock in the morning.

Apartment maintenance people do that for them. Mow the grass. It wasn't until Jimmy had been out of work for a month, sitting in a chair on their three-by-three square of lawn, shoulders hunched under his beige corduroy coat, his big hands passing a beer back and forth, that he exploded into the kitchen and announced that the maintenance people did a slipshod job. Their lines weren't straight. The hedges were scalped. A properly mowed lawn looked striped. Like a football field. Since then he'd planted tomatoes, hung spider plants and ferns all over the bathroom, even changed the little knobs on the kitchen cabinets.

"A man's got to sweat," he'd say, wiping his expanding forehead, as swollen and dazzling as the sun he shaded it from. "That's how he knows he's a man."

"Boil him," a woman from work advised. "My man stepped

out and I waited till he dozed off and put his hand in boiling water. Just like that. He be staying in."

"He's not cheating," Elsie said. "He just won't get a job."

"Not working. Stepping out. Same thing. Responsibility's responsibility. Boil him."

That the idea seemed tempting, unbelievably satisfying, terrified her.

Before Jimmy lost his job he was your typical five-o'clock six-packer. He came home bitching about his pea-brained manager or some asshole customer who thought he knew more about cars than a mechanic. He came home bone-tired, grease tattooed up his arms, his flesh damp and perfumed when he hugged her to him, cupped her rear. Sometimes he'd buy a couple of T-bones, and while she cooked dinner, he'd catcall knotty-lipped Lana Bleak, the news girl, and give beer to Felix until Elsie threatened to call the humane society. It was home, it was truth: the smell of grease and sweat and meat, Jimmy looking as if his body had been needed, laughing as he said, "Damn, that girl's got a mouth on her." Felix, with his wilting red bows and black-painted nails, careening around the apartment, bumping into the plaid couches until he threw up on Elsie's good carpet, and a grinning Jimmy said, "He's all right, El, the boy just needs to learn how to hold his liquor."

Laughter.

This new Jimmy scared her. She'd wake to find him in her kitchen, eggs smeared on his chest, buttered bread burning in the toaster. He shrank all the laundry. Dyed it pink. Bleached it until her feet went through the seat of her lacy underwear as if it were tissue. The newspapers piled up on the coffee table, the unemployment pages untouched.

It wasn't long before he shed his blue work shirts and Levis to dance around the house in tropical silk shirts and polyester blend pants with what hair he had slicked back, a sharp V of scalp shooting down his head.

"You've got to have a shtick," he'd say. "Personality. Personality's what gets you ahead in life."

Money's what got you ahead in life, and that's what Wayne had, and Elsie had Wayne and gave him up for Jimmy. Only Wayne didn't want the money. Hated his father for having it.

Wayne Chandler.

Even as a teenager Elsie knew there was something decadent, something forbidden and exotic about a man who possessed so much he had the luxury of wanting to give it away, the luxury of tormenting himself over his unfair advantage in life. A self-inflicted obsession. The depth of his darkness drove Elsie wild.

And his 1964 1/2 baby blue Mustang convertible didn't hurt. Elsie loved that car. Loved herself in it. The way the wind pulled through her hair. The other girls eyeing her like she'd stolen something of theirs. She'd shock herself by unbuttoning Wayne's pants when he was driving, pressing almost-shy lips to his crotch.

Wayne spent most of his time reading thick-skinned books by men whose names Elsie couldn't pronounce. He talked about enlightened consciousnesses and the plight of workers, the evils of capitalism and greed. Injustice, real or imagined, disabilitated him with passion. On their dates Elsie would carefully mention laid-off workers or companies crossing over borders or Wayne's father, who owned the car dealership and half the restaurants in town, and Wayne would work himself into a frenzy. Then Elsie might suggest he drive her up to Walnut Creek, where she hoped that frenzy would translate into them sliding sweaty over butter-slick seats. Instead he'd dance around the Mustang like a revival preacher, his curls icicle sharp with sweat, his index finger sharper, pointing at some imagined audience, while he sermonized on the horrors of corporations.

"You see that car?" he said once, looking in disgust at her beloved Mustang. "Do you know how many proletariats' backs that car rolled over? Do you?"

Elsie leaned into him, licked the salty place behind his ear, and whispered in a voice she thought to be low and sexy and witty, "I don't know about any proletariats, but you can roll me on my back in that Mustang any time."

He shoved her. "That's reprehensible Elsie. You're talking about people's lives."

He walked over to the car, stared at it for a moment, slammed his fist against the hood, then collapsed on it, his long legs swinging, his mind obviously not on seducing her. Elsie sat on the grass at his feet, listened to the creek breathing behind them. It embarrassed her, his rejection, made her worry if her lipstick was too bright, as he sometimes said, her hair too overdone, another common complaint. After a moment he looked her way, his eyes the glossed-over eyes of those drunk in the spirit, the same look that kept Elsie away from church, and said, "You're a product of your environment. That's all," which made Elsie picture herself rolling down a belt at the town mill. He leaned over, patted her on the head.

Then they fooled around, him making sounds like a small dog being stepped on.

It was on a night like this, Elsie barely seventeen, that Wayne asked her to run off and join the revolution in Central America. He said they could make a difference. That he needed her. That Central America needed her. That he was going to sell his Mustang to get down there, a symbolic sacrifice.

Just a month before, she'd met Jimmy McLain at a football game, older and knowing, a dark hook of hair lying dangerous on his forehead, a glint in his eye that promised he'd stride through her sure and clean, no crying and politics and preaching. If Jimmy had a Mustang, you could tell by the look of him he'd bend you all over it.

Elsie left Wayne for Jimmy, and Wayne left her for Central America.

Elsie and Jimmy were married a year later—quick in the preacher's home, just a cake and a picture of them kissing—on account of her pregnancy. Jimmy took the fake miscarriage harder than Elsie expected, slept curled around the miniature footballs and plastic bats he'd bought for the baby, his emotions so bare and real Elsie didn't know how to tell him they were based on a lie, even if she'd wanted.

He still brought her flowers on March fifteenth every year, the day she'd come screaming from the bathroom and told him she'd lost the baby. He imagined names for it. What if it was a girl? Maybe Elle. Or Eleanor. Or something else with an "E" like her mother. She'd be in ballet right now. Or softball. Or learning to cook. Maybe blue-eyed like Elsie. Maybe brown-eyed like Jimmy. Or a boy. Jimmy Jr. What Jimmy Sr. had hoped for when he'd bought all of those baseball bats, all those miniature footballs. And he'd be a quarterback. A ladies' man. Like his daddy. Only different. Better.

"He was our ticket, Elsie." Jimmy said this past year, "Our ticket to someplace different. Someplace else."

"Where?" Elsie asked.

"I don't know," Jimmy answered, his head pressed against her breasts. "Just somewhere other than this."

After fifteen years Elsie almost remembered their child as truth, too. Created fond memories of the baby they'd never had. A day in the park. A cake-smeared face. Jimmy's hand clutching a smaller one, the sun behind them erasing faces to white.

One afternoon after Jimmy had been out of work for a few months, Elsie came home from her job at Sears to find him stripped to his boxers, his mouth a panting "O," pale arms heaved overhead as if lifting a heavy object nowhere to be seen. When she asked him what he was doing, he said chopping wood. When she asked him where the wood was, he said it was spiritual, from his third-eye chakra. When she asked why he didn't cut the real wood sitting in the carport, he said the book didn't call for real wood. And when Elsie asked what book he was talking about, she opened a door she'd rather have left closed.

"It's the book that changed Levi's life," he said. "You know, after the divorce."

Elsie had known Levi Lancey since grade school. In the year since his wife left him for the bank teller in Eclectic, he'd shed his toupee and taken to wearing loose-knit Indian-print shirts with plummeting V necks showing off his oversized silver jewelry and oversized silver chest, a style which made him look as much like a pervert as when he'd worn a toupee and too-tight suits and a car salesman's mustache. And hippie clothes or not, he still got thrown in the can every Friday for passing out drunk in the parking lot of Harry's like he had for the last ten years, which was the reason his wife ran off with the bank teller in the first place.

From beneath the couch, Jimmy produced a slender blue book with a picture of a naked couple twisted into the shape of an infinity symbol on the cover. *Sextacy: Secrets of Love from Around the World.* He read from a passage titled "Splitting the Wood," an exercise to teach control and awareness in the bedroom. *A good way to fine-tune your hara is to split wood. Stand with your legs apart, your energy tight in your sex chakra and on the balls of your feet (solar plexus chakra). Take a deep breath, allow it to fill you, then exhale. Remember, you control your breathing. Now lift your arms over your head and make chopping motions. Don't forget to breathe out as you bend over, and in as you stand up. Repeat. Make Noise. This one is especially invigorating.*

"There's a whole stack of wood out there," Elsie said. "Couldn't you cut *and* breathe?"

"Yeah, well, I wanted to get it down this way first," Jimmy said. He let the book fall closed. "You know, focus on the breathing and the centering." His belly still trembled from the workout.

Hatred settled in Elsie's throat like a chokehold. She couldn't breathe.

"I need a hobby," she said. Something of her own. Watercolors or ceramics. She didn't care. A class on soufflés would work. She needed to get out of this house.

The only class at the local community college that worked with her schedule was yoga, which made Jimmy deliriously happy, as he was all about the spiritual these days. If Elsie were in therapy, which she didn't exactly believe in and couldn't afford even if she did, they might've said her telling the women at yoga her name was Chantel Lovell was a bad sign. After walking into the gas station turned minigym and paying the five-dollar fee, she noticed she didn't recognize any of her girlfriends' faces out of the soft-hipped women squatting on their mats, little islands of calm floating about in the ease of foreign music. All of her friends had three kids or three ex-husbands to deal with, some of them both, and none had time to sit Indian-style and hum for an hour. These yoga women—mostly young students at the community college—were wrapped like leftovers in transparent scarves and shiny leotards, their skin so sheer and soft it looked filtered through a screen. The women Elsie knew mapped their lives with their faces, and since these yoga women looked clean-scraped, she figured

pool and a maid, although she would choose a stodgy woman, perhaps with thick ankles, a guttural German accent.

On her lunch break she went to the mall bookstore and asked the saleslady for a book on revolution. The saleslady reluctantly sold her a copy of the *The Communist Manifesto*, eyeing her suspiciously, as if Elsie were planning an uprising, an assembly of the oppressed, a group of which the pinched-lip, makeup-streaked saleslady mistakenly, Elsie thought, did not find herself a member.

When Elsie got home Jimmy had on his favorite tropical shirt— white flowers the size of a palm, their petals spread like fingers, the background a vivid, Miracle-Gro blue. He'd made grilled chicken breasts, glazed carrots, and steamed broccoli. There was chocolate mousse for dessert and nothing had burned. He'd even twisted real linen napkins into miniature teepees, a trick he'd gotten off the Internet. Felix was still nowhere to be found.

"Got a job yet?" Elsie said, pushing her carrots around her plate.

He ignored her. Said, "You know what I've been thinking? I've been thinking that maybe my getting laid off is a blessing. That maybe I should take some classes down at the community college. Some computer classes. There's tons of computer jobs in the paper. Or maybe study some accounting. Somebody somewhere's got to have some money to manage."

"I hate carrots," Elsie said, thrusting her plate in front of her so hard that one of the carrots rolled right off onto the table like a fluorescent log.

"It wouldn't take but a couple of years. I could work nights as a mechanic. A side job."

"How much was that bottle of wine?" Elsie asked, pointing at the cheap bottle they'd finished. "You know we can't afford extras with you out of work."

Jimmy quit talking, eased up behind Elsie, and coiled his hands around her shoulders kneading. "You're tense," he said.

Lately, Jimmy'd been pushing her to do various positions out of his spiritual sex books. He'd ask her to straddle him, both of them sitting up, and achieve genital union without movement. He called this position YabYum, told her they were a hieroglyph of flesh. Hieroglyph? He tried to get Elsie to hold her hand against his heart and breath out to him breathing into her. Told her he was thrusting his light into her, through her genitals, up her back, and out her crown chakra. But that's not what Elsie wanted thrust into her, and when she would say this half-joking, he would push her off him and sleep on the couch.

Tonight he twirled her to the den, flipped on Al Green, raised her hand as if she were a prom queen, bowed short and curt, his newly growing potbelly swelling out when he bent, his bald head glistening, and asked may he have this dance. Elsie tried to tell herself that she was being ridiculous, a horrible person, that she'd married for better or worse and she could have done a lot worse than Jimmy. But when he ran his hands up and down her back, massaging her kidneys like his books told him to do, she felt as if he were going to burrow inside her, those too-clean hands picking their way, past knobby vertebrae, past bone-fingered ribs, past the long globe of stomach, sinking into the gore of her.

"I feel sick," she said.

"Too much wine?"

Elsie wanted him to tease her like he did when they were young and, more often than not, silly drunk, her inevitably unable to hold her liquor and throwing up outside the door of his truck or in the bathroom sink. He'd tell her to make sure she brushed her teeth before coming to bed. They'd laugh and make crude jokes and there would be nothing but the nakedness of want and youth, and then later, aging bodies, no fancy words to hide behind, words that he'd been using lately, words like *yoni* or *lingam* or *chakra* or *hara*.

Jimmy went into the kitchen to get her an ice pack, made a big affair of fixing her a comfortable place on the couch, and began rubbing her feet, pressing deeply with his thumb in the middle of her left sole until she howled in pain and asked him what the hell he was doing.

"It's called the Kidney One," he said. "Acupressurists say it's the spot that revitalizes sexual vigor."

"Since when has my kidney been in my foot?" she snapped.

He looked disappointed that he'd failed at the foot massage. Elsie wanted to comfort him, but comforting him might lead to other things, and Elsie wasn't prepared to go there. He went back to rubbing her feet until he fell asleep, his head, globed and tanned like Wayne's Mexican maid's ass, pressing into her belly. She was wide-awake.

Each morning for the next week, Elsie skipped breakfast, told Jimmy she was working overtime, and rode up to Charlie's Diner and parked close enough to watch Wayne work. Elsie knew his schedule as well as she knew her cycle. He had one egg, sunny side up, a slice of toast with strawberry jam, sometimes grape, and two cups of coffee between six-thirty and seven-thirty. Then he chewed on a cigar, a habit he must have picked up in Central America, but never lit it. Then he thumbed through papers, marking them with his gnawed pencil. She didn't know what he did after that because she had to go to work, and if she was late one more time, her boss said she was fired.

After Sears on Mondays, Wednesdays, and Fridays, instead of going to yoga, she did the same thing. When she finished her shift, Elsie would go into the Sears bathroom and transform into Chantel so Jimmy wouldn't suspect anything. She'd spent a good portion of her paycheck on supplementing her Chantel wardrobe. Added fiery red leg warmers to match her favorite shade of lipstick, hot pink ones to bring out the blush of her skin. Bought layers of see-through scarves and a book on how to tie them. A saucy knot at the neck. A twist around the chest for a halter-top. Her leotards had advanced from the first old black one to a wicked fuchsia or dangerous silver, the legs cut high to her waist, the fleshiness of her hips bulging slightly at the top. With each layer she added, the sexier, the more rebellious she felt. And when she imagined Wayne imagining her, as she hoped he had done for all these years, she imagined him pleased.

She drove back to Charlie's and parked. Sometimes, if she couldn't see Wayne from the parking lot, she pulled out her copy of the *Manifesto* and read and reread it, making small marks in the margins by passages she felt would spawn conversation between Wayne and herself. She practiced phrases in the car, letting the exotic words roll off her tongue, words like *bourgeoisie* and *spectre* and *beaux esprits*. She imagined herself strolling into the diner, sliding into Wayne's booth, linking one sexy leg-warmer-clad leg over the other, leaning onto Wayne as if they were picking up a conversation that had ended only moments before, asking *On what foundation is the present family, the bourgeois family, based?* His eyes would glaze in rapture like in high school, and Elsie would be responsible for his rebirth, the regeneration of that pointing, sermonizing finger.

If she was late getting home, Elsie told Jimmy she had been out looking for Felix, going door to door, passing out the flyers Jimmy made on the computer. "See," he said when he handed them to her. "I think I've got a knack with computers. I really should take those classes." She tacked a few around the apartment building and shoved the rest under the front seat of her car along with the McDonald's wrappers and Sweet 'n Low packets.

But Elsie usually made it home in time to gnaw on Jimmy's burnt-up pork chops or chicken legs until her mouth was full of hate, afterward trying to keep Jimmy out of her, who by now had a nice stack of self-help books on his bedside table. *How to Put the Juice Back in Your Marriage. 101 Nights of Love. The Art of Making Sex Sacred. The Angry Marriage: Overcoming the Rage and Reclaiming the Love. Asian Secrets of Sexual Ecstasy: Discover the Power of Bliss. The Encyclopedia of Sacred Sexuality: From Aphrodisiacs and Exstasy to Yoni Worship and Zap-Lam Yoga. The Cosmic Embrace: An Illustrated Guide to Sacred Sex.*

Sometimes it was easier to give in than to listen to him read out of those books, so she would close her eyes and imagine that Jimmy was Wayne in Central America, a radical, guns wrapped around his naked hips, a blood red bandana tied around his forehead. He was wounded, possibly mortally, and the last act he wanted to perform was making wild love to her while roaring revolutionary cries. *Down with the bourgeoisie! Abolition of the family!* If she managed to ignore Jimmy's loose belly slapping into hers, she was so responsive he whirled about the apartment the next morning, flipping through the employment pages of the newspaper, whistling.

One November evening, Felix gone for over a month, Elsie sat watching Wayne long after she usually went home, unable to face another evening with Jimmy. The sun had burned down to the edges of the asphalt hours ago, and Elsie had put her book away, too scared to turn on the interior lights for fear someone would notice her and mistake her for a weirdo or a stalker. She watched

Wayne refill water and tea and coffee to patrons with raised hands, most of them drained from a too-long day or a too-long life and not bothering to look his way. Elsie was lost in the quiet of her night, the moving scenery of the diner, its familiar warmth.

Elsie went to put the *Manifesto* in the glove compartment, and when she looked back up the spongy, gray geriatric patrons had begun growing jaunty mustaches, flashing steeled smiles as menacing as bared razor blades, their limbs fleshing and pulsing with virtuous anger. The smoker-thin, bleached-blonde women of indeterminable age had shed their permed curls for colored turbans, their weedy arms raised to angry fists above their head in protest, no longer asking for more tea or coffee but for truth, for justice, for revolution. It was a meeting of the exploited, of the oppressed, and Wayne was at the center, wielding guns like exclamation points in his beautiful, serious hands.

Elsie succumbed to the passion of the mob before her. She worked a hand under her leotard and found a nipple, pinching hard, the burn roaring to her belly. The other hand found its way to her crotch, where she imagined her finger as the barrel of Wayne's gun. Although she tried to push it from her mind, Jimmy's description of her *yoni*, her lotus flower he'd called it, kept rearing its hideous, petaled head, and the more she fought it, trying to replace the wilting flower with metal and gunpowder, the more vivid the image became until she clawed at herself in frustration, so intent on what she was doing she didn't hear the knock on her car window.

A brick tower of a police officer stood outside, trying to see in the window. She had no idea how long he'd been standing there.

"Pig," she muttered, rolling down the window. It seemed appropriate.

When he asked her to step out of the car, she poked one pink leg warmer calf out of the car door, looked around the parking lot making sure no one was watching, and stood in front of the officer.

"This is a family establishment," he said.

"I'm part of a family," she replied, looking him in the face so she didn't seem guilty. He had one of those thick, dripping mustaches you see on cops on TV.

When he asked what she'd been doing parked there for the last three hours, she pointed to under her car seat where the crumpled flyers were and told him she was looking for her dog, going around asking people if they'd seen him. He pulled out a flyer. Felix's tongue wagged from the picture.

"Hard to ask people if they've seen your dog when you don't get out of the car, don't you think?" This was what Wayne used to call a rhetorical question.

The officer eyed her trench coat and pink leg warmers, her gypsy scarves tied around her forehead. It was cold so she was hopping from foot to foot, and her bells jingled like something breaking. She knew he'd decided to take her in.

The patrons, their bodies their bodies again, began gathering at the window of the diner to see what was going on in the parking lot. As she rode off in the back of the police car, she thought she might have seen Wayne in the diner window, his cigar clutched in his mouth like Castro, his fingers humming against his narrow hips, his head nodding in approval.

Jimmy wouldn't look at her when he bailed her out. They walked to his truck in silence.

They barreled down Main Street, past the Feed and Seed, past Bill's Dollar Store, the new McDonald's a blur of yellow and red, and still they picked up speed.

"Felix came back today," he said.

"Really?" she said, "that's good."

"He's pretty messed up. Some SOB sprayed him with buckshot. I'm thinking he might've been hanging around somebody's bitch. But still, who would do that to a fifteen-pound poodle wearing bows, huh?"

Elsie shrugged. She tried to feel great sorrow for Felix, but she could barely remember what he looked like.

"I was about to carry him to the vet when the station called," Jimmy said. "I'd saved up a bit of money from doing odd jobs that I was going to use for a computer class. To surprise you. Even so I was glad to have it to get Felix patched up."

Elsie didn't respond. Jimmy shifted to a higher gear.

"But then the station calls and says that my wife was picked up for disorderly conduct. That it should be lewd and lascivious behavior, but since this was her first offense, they were going to go easy."

The only sound the thump of the road beneath them, which was passing far more quickly than it should.

"And where was my wife picked up, I asked. You know what they said, Elsie? Said your wife was picked up in front of Wayne Chandler's diner. That a concerned citizen who had seen her there every other afternoon for a while now turned her in. So guess where my computer money and Felix's vet money went. Guess."

This was another one of those rhetorical questions.

"It went towards bailing my perverted wife out of jail."

What she wanted to say was, *I'm a pervert? Me?* What about him and all his weird sex books? That if he'd had a steady job, he could afford night classes *and* vet bills. That if he took care of things she wouldn't be rubbing herself in front of Charlie's Diner.

But she was not in much of an arguing position, so she muttered a sorry that provoked him into driving faster.

"Sorry?" he said. "Yeah, you're sorry all right."

When the truck jerked to a stop in front of their apartment, Jimmy didn't get out, just stared through the windshield. "Where'd we go wrong, El?" he finally said. "Maybe if the baby had come everything would be different, you know?"

She left him alone in the truck.

Inside Felix curled tight on a blanket in the kitchen, his cottonball hair seeping red, one eye rolling loose and bloodied in its socket, the other glazed over like a pastry. He made a wet, whimpering sound when she touched him. He looked well fed, and Elsie assumed someone in the neighborhood had taken care of him until he'd wandered into the wrong yard.

Jimmy passed both of them when he came in. She could hear him rattling around in the utility room. After a few minutes he came back with a shovel and a pistol.

"Come on," he said, nodding to the back door of the apartment where their little square of grass was.

Elsie pulled Felix into her lap. He howled and nipped at her hands.

"What're you going to do?" she asked, already knowing. "You can't shoot a dog. That's inhumane. Especially not Felix. And not in an apartment complex. You'll get arrested."

"You're on such friendly terms with the cops. You explain it," he said.

She picked Felix up and carried him outside. Poor Felix, his meaty tongue roiling in his mouth, one eye given up, the other no longer his own to control. When she pictured Jimmy wielding a gun like a revolutionary, this was not the scene she envisioned, but whatever was?

Jimmy dug a hole in the grass he'd so meticulously mowed over the last few months. He was sweating so much that in spite of the raw cold of the November night, he took off his shirt and threw it on the ground. Each time Jimmy placed his booted foot on the edge of the shovel for leverage, leaning over and pressing down with pogo-stick-like jumps, the curdled flesh of his belly waved and rippled and his gelled hair hung stiffly over his forehead as if saluting the night. Elsie wanted to smooth his hair back, wanted to cover his pitiful belly, wanted to hide the starkness of it all. The only sounds were the crunch of earth against metal and Felix, wet-breathed and cooing.

When Jimmy finished, he retrieved his shirt and spread it in the middle of the hole, motioning for Elsie to place Felix on it.

"He's already dead," she said.

"Dead?" Jimmy stuck two fingers against Felix's neck. Paused. Wiped the blood on his jeans. "Bastards," he said, patting Felix's head.

He stuck the pistol into the waistband of his jeans, turned the expanse of his back to her—the milk white of the November moon—waved a dirt-covered hand toward the shovel, told her to clean up the mess, and walked back into their apartment with the old familiar body-worn gait.

Elsie knew he would sit on the couch and flip through the channels while she made dinner. In the morning he would get up and look through the classifieds and find a job at another garage. And he would come home tired as he always had, only now there would be no cupping her rear with grease-stained hands or teasing about knotty-lipped Lana Bleak until one day there was.

Elsie arranged Felix, his bowed ears flipped back, his pink perforated belly oozing oil-slick wet onto Jimmy's favorite shirt—a pattern of sleek, colorless flowers opening to blue.

The One Thing
God'll Give You

Any time a man took off from Tallassee, his woman's money or car or TV or hope along with him, my momma would look at me, hiss her eyes narrow, say, There's one thing you can count on from a man, and that's him leaving. My momma should have been a drinking woman considering, but she wasn't.

My Willie ain't that kind of man, I told her. And he doesn't have a car, so how would he go about leaving if he wanted?

That kind of man? she said laughing, shooting spit out of her beautiful piano-key gap. Hula, there ain't but one kind of man.

Momma would have known. She'd met him twenty times over.

They said to her, Addie, I'm going to get you off your feet and out of that bar. They said, Addie, I'm going to take you places you've never been. They said, Addie baby, I'm going to treat you like a queen.

The last one named himself Fast Eddie, which I thought was dangerous until I met ten men in the next ten years who called themselves Fast Eddie. Only this Fast Eddie played pool by popping the cue ball into the pocket and cursing God and cursing the pool stick and then saying it wasn't his night and going back to doing what he was good at—drinking whiskey straight.

When my momma worked days, Fast Eddie and me would sit on the front porch, me in Momma's rocker, him perched on the wide ledge, his long booted legs linked over the railing like a kid on a pier, a guitar in his lap. I'd snap beans for dinner and he'd dip (Hula, he'd say, you can always judge a man by his dip. Copenhagen means he's got balls; Skoal means he's a pussy), sip whiskey from the bottle and pluck out Elvis or Willie. Every now and then he'd sing along to a sad part about dying or loss or love, which I learned later are all one and the same, and say, That's real, Hula, do you hear that? That's real feeling. You remember that.

Other times we talked about life and the meaning of it all. Eddie told me once, Hula, it's your choice to live or die. Like I get to pick the way and the when of how I go. Like if some big bus came barreling down on me I could just put out my hand and say, No sir, I ain't going today. I got laundry to do.

Eddie believed it, but said if by chance the Lord called, he wanted us to perch him up on that big bike of his, pop a cigarette in his mouth and light it, make sure to stock cold beer in the saddlebag, and then douse him with gasoline and set him off to the other world blazing. Said this was Native American–like but modern.

We never figured out if he avoided dying or not because he took off on his bike without the to-do. Momma said he was sure enough good for dying, and that if she ever got her hands on him, she'd prove it. Eddie took her entire week's paycheck. But more than that, he took her wood-carving tools, took them and not the TV. Guess it's hard to tote a TV on a bike, and if you're drunk enough those tools might look like something of worth. And they were to Momma, though I never actually saw her finish a piece in my life, just scratch out a half of a horse or a hint of an angel late at night, which is what I said when she started crying. She said it's not that she used the tools, it's that she *could* have used them, and when your *could* is gone, what's left?

I was in tenth grade, just sixteen, when I started dating Willie.
You got a good head on your shoulders, my momma said. A
shame to waste it. Remember that.

I tried to remember. I made straight A's and got my name on the
bulletin board in Winston High Lobby and my picture taken for
the yearbook and the *Tallassee Record*, a bunch of skinny, tiny-
breasted girls straddling gym bleachers, a few boys in the shadows.

But Willie. He said I had me a good ass on me. A high ass. The
kind of ass somebody would want to eat lunch from, and it would
be a shame to waste that, too.

Momma worked with Willie down at the Rodeo Club where he
bussed tables and kept things neat. He always smelled like that
spray they wash tables down with, real clean and sharp. Had gray
eyes near the size of quarters and dark hair that curled against his
neck in upside-down question marks.

Willie liked to take toothpicks from the bar and build things on
his breaks, little forts and bridges and houses with perfect miniature everything.

That's how we got together, him asking me to help and listening to my ideas. One day he made a little toothpick sign that said
Willie and Hula's and hung it on one of his houses, and before
you know it, that's what we became, Willie and Hula, one name
hooked to the other.

Hula, Momma'd say, slanting her lids at Willie, keep your eyes
off boys and on them books.

But Willie, he taught me different things.

Said, Hula, your eyes are sky blue, bluer than that.

Said, Hula, your ass is round as a basketball, bouncy too.

I know that doesn't sound romantic, but Willie loved basketball, so it really was sweet.

Said, Hula, you taste like honey, girl, pure honey.

My momma worked down at the Rodeo Club most nights, but
she wasn't the kind of woman you'd expect. Sometimes she waited
tables and slung beers, but mainly she took care of the numbers

and the money in the little room with the *Employees Only* on the door. It made me feel important when I was little to go and color in that room, because I knew just nobody could go in. Mr. Bill, the owner (who some thought was light in the boots on account of his lisp and the fact he never married and because he only wore pastel shirts), gave me little pink and purple umbrellas they stuck in the drinks on Rodeo Luau night, when all the wannabe cowboys came in with their worn-down boots and worn-down smiles knocking up against all the worn-down women at the bar, fumbling to get their fruit-colored leis over their heads without taking off their cowboy hats or baseball caps. They'd offer their leis to girls, ask, "Hey, you been lei'd yet tonight?" laughing beer all over.

I'd take those little umbrellas and twirl them in front of my face like I'd seen dancers do with real umbrellas on TV, but they were too small to do the trick, so mainly I just stuck them behind my ears and danced Hawaiian style. That's how I got myself the name Hula, even though Tallassee's a life away from Hawaii, which I always read as a sign I'd be leaving this town. And since they named me down at the Rodeo Club, it was almost as if they were family, and I used to say if I ever got married, I'd have Mr. Bill, queer or not, give me away, big cowboy hat and dipping tobacco and pink tux if he wanted, have him walk me down the aisle white and pearled, since my daddy wasn't there to do the job.

Daddy left when I was barely five. He was a big man, my daddy, pillowing and open-armed. I liked him. Liked the way he held me on his lap and read *Green Eggs and Ham*. Liked the way he'd give me sips of his Budweiser until my head got foggy and dreamy and *Green Eggs and Ham* didn't live in the book anymore but in my head like cartoon dreams. Liked the way he cupped Momma's rear with his big hands, not dirty, but sweet like it was precious. Liked the way he made her giggle girlish, spit bubbling and hissing against her piano tooth gap.

Momma always missed him. You could tell because she refused to say his name. She never talked about the stuff she used to like but couldn't have any more, like Daddy and her schooling and her art. But I heard her crying when she got home from the club, knew she craved some late at night and kept those glossy-paged art books under her bed, along with her poems full of mountains and streams that weren't streams but rumbling thoughts that flowed

into words or bodies and the meaning of bodies speaking without speaking none.

In the middle of those poems, she kept a long tail-like wa of white blonde hair, as white as light, because that was wh used to have before there was me and Daddy and then only

When Momma died I took those poems and those picture: to Auburn and had them framed. I hung them in my living next to little Hula's school pictures. My favorite is this eagl ing in sky over a lake because you can't separate the sky fron lake, can't tell where things end and others begin.

All men don't leave.

That's what I told Momma when she found out I was se Willie.

Look at Uncle Jerry, I said. And Mr. Teeney. They're still arou

Uncle Jerry stayed with my Aunt Beanie for more than decades. Momma said Uncle Jerry stayed because he didn't h legs from drag racing even though Aunt Beanie told him ti and time again to quit pouring money into that souped-up M tang, and he ignored her until he hit that tree stoned as a monl and lost his legs, so how was he going to go anywhere nohow

Besides, Uncle Jerry never worked a day that I can rememb and Aunt Beanie was always crying when we were little that t babies needed diapers and the babies needed food and she had had her hair done right in years. At least after the accident he dre disability and couldn't get around too good in his wheelchair he wasn't much trouble, just wheeled off in the corner of tl kitchen or in front of the TV.

Aunt Beanie said the best thing he'd ever done for that famil was to get rid of them legs. Said it with him sitting right ther watching her, sad cause he'd found the Lord and Aunt Beanie' stopped looking. Momma said when you can't get up and go no where, about the only thing left to find is the Lord.

What Aunt Beanie found was a man out at the mill.

This was a few years after my Willie. Leslie Owens. A rough sort on account of the girl name. That went on for half a decade, and after a while Leslie came right on up to Aunt Beanie's house

and ate dinner, sometimes sleeping over, Uncle Jerry sitting there in the corner, nodding off or reading the Bible or praying crazy or eating TV dinners in the living room in front of *Dallas* reruns.

Uncle Jerry drowned himself in the tub one Easter morning, which goes to show what they tell you about two inches of water is true. At the funeral Aunt Beanie cried a lot and cursed that Mustang and cursed fate, but I heard her say insurance don't pay on suicides and she hoped to get it ruled accidental.

Remember that, Hula, Momma said on the way home from the funeral. It's a sad thing life does to a woman. Makes her practical and unapologetic for it.

And Mr. Teeney.

Mr. Teeney was my high school biology teacher's husband. He and Mrs. Teeney came together to football games each Friday, waved their skinny black and gold pompoms and huddled close under blankets and stood up when we scored and screamed Go Bobcats! then sat back down as quick as they could, looking uncomfortable touching.

Well, Momma said, Mr. Teeney's out all hours at the Rodeo Club rubbing that nice-guy smile over girls about the age Mrs. Teeney teaches. So you see, she said, there are many ways to leave a woman.

Although I didn't tell Momma at the time because there would have been explaining, all the kids knew about Mr. Teeney and his women. But Mrs. Teeney still came to school early and perky-faced with her church pumps and her pleated wool skirts tucked tight under her thighs and a tighter smile tucked on her face and everyone knowing that her husband was knowing everyone.

Mrs. Teeney was my favorite in school because she cared and you felt it. She drove over to Auburn and bought books the state couldn't afford, would copy the whole thing twenty times over with her own money. We all kind of felt like her kids, the kids we figured she couldn't have because she didn't have any.

In biology when we started talking about reproduction it was hard for me not to see Mrs. Teeney in that drawing of canals and ovaries and wombs, not to see her insides as dark and endless, gnawed out and bottomless so nothing stuck, just poured through her whiskey-smooth. Hard for me not to imagine Momma's as

endless too, endless in a different way, because I stuck and my daddy didn't.

To teach us responsibility, Mrs. Teeney made us carry around flour babies. She made the boys carry one too. Al Sims, who was rumored to have three balls and real macho for it, said he didn't see why he had to carry around some baking doll because there wasn't no way on God's green earth he could have himself a baby. But Mrs. Teeney, she stuck to her guns, said he had a part in the process as well, and if he wanted details, he should go to chapter six of our biology book. Then she made us paint a face on the pretend babies and paste yarn to their heads and dress them in our baby clothes left over.

I named mine Cheyenne. That's where I planned on going when I graduated. I gave her blue eyes with yellow yarn hair, because I hoped if I had one it would be looking like me.

After two weeks Mrs. Teeney showed us a video of a woman in childbirth, showed it to all of us, boys and girls, the camera focusing right on that woman's hot pink privates. Afterwards I told Mrs. Teeney that there ain't no better birth control than watching a woman get split wide open with a squished-up baby head.

That weekend Momma made biscuits and a chocolate cake out of Cheyenne, and I giggled the whole time eating, thinking if you're going to have a baby in your belly, this was the best way to do it.

———

It happened like it always happens.

Said, Hula, your shoulder tastes like cotton candy. Pure spun sugar.

Said, Hula, your pussy feels like a glove of fire.

After we fooled around, we used to go get us a shake and a hamburger and some fries. Willie dipped his fries in his shake like catsup, making me love him all the more. Willie, he paid for all of it. And I thought he was a good man and had himself a job and when he saved up enough money, we were moving to Cheyenne. He was going to get himself a pair of cowboy boots and was going to be a ranch hand like in Clint Eastwood movies, or maybe build fancy houses hanging off hills like you see in magazines. In the winters we were going up to the mountains where I would teach skiing like in the Olympics because I loved mountains and snow even though I'd never seen them. Some things you just think you know.

Willie, he threw up on my feet when I told him.

Said, Hula, you sure it's mine?

Then he said he was sorry, that I was his girl and he'd get another job and we'd raise this baby the right way, that he'd be a better daddy than my daddy or his daddy or any of the daddies we knew.

I said I hope it'd be blonde and blue-eyed like me.

Willie, he said he hoped that too, because the only thing better than one Hula is two Hulas.

I said if it's a girl we're going to name it Cheyenne.

Then we did it real slow like and sweet but without a rubber or worry, because I figured you couldn't get no more pregnant than pregnant.

My momma started waiting up for me when she wasn't working, her hair and clothes smelling of smoke and whiskey, but her breath clean. She barely touched a drop. Said, Hula, don't you touch that stuff. It doesn't take you to a better world, just keeps you in the one you're in for good. Then she'd wink and tell me how I got here, her and daddy drinking a bit too much and then before she knew it *boom*. The boom always sounded like a car crash.

But she left out what her poems tell, the beauty and the body whispering and how lovely and how tragic it all is. That's what I thought about when I thought about Willie, all her poems about love I'd found, all those poems about how Daddy made her body feel when his body was inside hers.

Sometimes I wonder about that, my daddy inside my momma, her barely sixteen, her insides, where I spilt from, my daddy's heat searching. I wonder if deep down in her belly she'd wished I hadn't stuck. What if? What if I had tumbled out without her knowing when she'd bled one month, just a bad idea, a defect her body took care of like Mrs. Teeney told us bodies do, and her ignorant of the whole thing, ignorant and being a girl just a bit longer.

Momma had me at sixteen. Next to the pictures of little Hula and Momma's paintings is a picture of Momma in a flowered Sunday dress with her long white hair wrapped in a bun at her neck. She looks petrified. Daddy has his arm, thick and tanned, slung about her stiff shoulders, one side of his mouth tugged into a grin like he'd won something. It's their wedding picture. I'm in her, tight and balled and buried and forever, only there's no hint of me in the curve of her belly. How terrified she must have been, her life rearranging and deciding for a thing she couldn't even see yet, a thing they told her existed but she couldn't hold in her hands.

I didn't know how to tell Momma, but it turned out I didn't have to because I kept throwing up mornings. Bacon, I threw up. Coffee, I threw up. Toast, I threw up. After a week a light turned on in Momma's head and she came into the bathroom whipping my head back with a fistful of hair making me mess all over myself.

Oh Hula, she said, tell me no.

She looked like I'd hit her, or like she wanted to hit me. Then she stood up, shook her head, and left me on the bathroom floor.

When Momma came back later that night she smelled of whiskey I knew she didn't hardly touch and her voice laid low and smooth. She pulled me on her lap, little-girl-like, even though I'm a good head taller because I get my height from my daddy. She started talking about responsibilities and souls and doing things for the better of everyone and after a few minutes I caught on that Momma was trying to get rid of my baby. So I told her right then and there that I was old enough to get myself pregnant and old enough to decide to get unpregnant.

She said, Hula, you don't know what this world can do to you. It takes a lifetime to lose religion and that's the one thing God'll give you in the end.

I prayed something like this:

Dear Lord, I'm not much on getting rid of babies because I know a soul's a soul and You know every hair on our head before we've even got a head, and right's right and wrong's wrong. To tell you the truth, even though You already know this because You knew what I was thinking before I was thinking it, I couldn't imagine killing me and Willie's baby, so that's not what I'm asking. But Mrs. Teeney says that if something isn't right with the baby that the body'll often take care of it on its own, just naturally clean it on out. Now I'm not saying that I want you to take a perfectly good baby and make it defected, but maybe if somebody else is supposed to be having a defected one, maybe some older lady like Mrs. Teeney who doesn't got much time left for babies, You could switch them out and let mine wait just a bit longer in heaven until after I've got myself a degree and a ski teaching certificate. It ain't like a soul's got a shelf life. And if that's wrong, I take it all back and please don't let me die or get hit by a bus or get my face scarred for being selfish. It's just an idea, but I know You know best. From this moment on, I am going to depend on Jesus for my salvation. Amen.

I'll tell you this, God's not always listening, because a month later I was still pregnant and Momma was still coming home whiskey doused. When I tried to call Willie, his momma said he couldn't come to the phone. Then one day I called and she said he had took off, not in his car, because like I said he didn't have one, but his grandma's car which he stole.
My baby's daddy a thief. What a way to start.
Is he coming back? I asked. I thought maybe he'd gone to make more money, gone to make a better life for me and the baby.
I'm sure he is, Honey, she said, but we both knew better.

One morning early, still dark outside, I felt a hand on my shoulder, smelled my mother's smell, Dove and White Shoulders, her breath clean, her thin silhouette cut against the night, beautiful, like a shadowed mist.
Baby, I just hate to see it. I just hate to see it all start for you now. You understand? she said, her hand against my forehead. Then my light flipped on, and there my momma was, a pair of my jeans and a T-shirt in her hands. You understand, she said, You understand we're going to Birmingham to take care of this.
The only sound hearts *boom, boom* pulsing.
She straddled me. We flipped on the floor, my arm knocking the lamp over. She got the T-shirt wrapped tight around my neck and

blue jeans stuck on my ankles. She tumbled out of my room, her robe hanging off her shoulders, one tit squished out from under her bra. Then I heard a particular kind of click. I'd lived in the country long enough to know that kind of click, and there was Momma, standing right in my doorway with a shotgun cocked and pointed at my head, her mouth pinched, determined, her hair dancing alive, her legs stabbed firm in the floor. She looked like a superhero, a she-warrior.

You're going to Birmingham, she said. You hear me?

I heard her.

The whole way there I hoped the police would stop her for swerving or that we'd need gas and I could pass a note to the cashier with something like, HELP, MY MOMMA'S TRYING TO SHOOT ME AND MY BABY, which might have looked strange seeing as how I didn't have a baby yet and my stomach didn't show one.

But we didn't stop and the police didn't stop us. Momma, her hair a mess of platinum spikes, still wore her bathrobe.

She only spoke once.

Hula, she said, you know why I had you? Why I wanted you? Why I let your daddy put you in me? Why I planned it?

The *boom* in her stories that made me always sounded accidental, like two bodies bumping into each other with mumbled sorrys lost in night and bodies speaking words without speaking none.

I wanted God to give me something I could keep, she said. Something of mine that couldn't be taken away. And He did. You understand what I'm saying?

This is what I understood: God was surely a man, and every woman knew it.

When we got to the clinic, Momma parked close to the door so she could see it, told me to go on in, that she was going to be sitting in the car with the gun and if I tried to run off or didn't stay in long enough don't think she wouldn't use it.

Then she said, Hula, you know I love you don't you? So hurt, my momma.

The building was plain brown brick, like a dentist's office. Inside everything smelled clean and sharp like Willie's smell, which made me miss him and then hate him and his heat always pushing against me. There were men huddled in seats twisting fingers and women reading magazines or rocking babies in their laps and the TV mounted on the wall had Donahue talking. All in all, it wasn't nearly as bad as I thought it would be.

I had to wait in line for a while because of the crowd. I guess Saturday, being the weekend, is a busy time for them. When I got to the counter, a blonde woman in a sweater with sewn-on horses wearing glitter saddles reminding me of out West and Cheyenne smiled tight and practiced. She was young and fat and only getting fatter.

I don't want to be doing this, I said.

She smiled that same tight smile.

Precounseling's part of the fee, she said. You got an appointment?

I don't know, I answered.

She looked annoyed. Said, What's your name?

Hula Hawkin, I said, and her lumpy white fingers started flying on the keyboard.

I leaned real close to her so the people behind me couldn't hear and whispered, Momma, she's got a gun.

Those white fingers went stiff as death. She turned around looking for someone to run this by and no one was near so she said, What do you mean she's got a gun? This is not a joking matter.

In the parking lot, I said. She's got herself a gun out in the car.

I tried to tell the fat lady that Momma didn't intend to hurt nobody, and if she did, nobody but me, but she'd pushed some siren, was screaming at the guards to go to the parking lot.

Which car? she said. Where is she?

I said, Wait a minute, lady. You got the wrong idea.

No one listened. The children screamed and the mothers and the soon-to-be-not mothers hid under chairs and the whole place throbbed with that siren and I thought I was going to be sick.

I ran to the parking lot to try to tell Momma she better take off or hide that gun, but they already had her out of the car, her face pressed against asphalt, her legs splayed open so you could see the soft part of her near the top of her thighs, their rough hands moving over her pale skin, her bathrobe thrown from her, showing her matching satin bra and panties.

I called to her. She closed her eyes so she couldn't see me, so I disappeared.

After a few hours they let me have the car to get myself back home, and when I-459 hit Highway 280, I thought of not taking it, of maybe turning around and heading back to that clinic and getting myself cleaned out. But I'm not as strong as my momma and I knew it even then. I thought of not turning east back toward Tallassee, of taking that car and turning it west, west to possibility, west to mountains with mansions clinging to them like kudzu, west to snow skiing and real cowboys, not the wannabe cowboys at the club, but thick-skinned cowboys who face the elements, who rust out in the workday sun to a ruddy, well-used brown color.

I was on the off-ramp to 280 east without realizing which way I'd gone, not even feeling that steering wheel in my fingers, just hummed into silence by the *thunk* of the road beneath me.

Momma died with Little Hula and a book spread on her lap.

I'd found her three years before in the *Employees Only* room mumbling words that weren't words, her face slacked soft and somewhere else.

Hu-wa, she called me after that. Hu-wa, wha a uh?

You're here, Momma, I said. At home.

She was smoothed beautiful those last years, her face forgetting what she told me to remember, her body slight and fragile like glass you put high so fingers can't touch.

Me and Aunt Beanie and Hula were planning breakfast on the back patio at Momma's, where me and Hula lived to make sure Momma did.

Aunt Beanie and me were cutting potatoes in the kitchen, talking about the men who were our men at the time, the things they said to make our bellies dip low and hot.

Hula had been reading to her Grandma in her wheelchair out back, *Green Eggs and Ham*, her favorite and my favorite, and she'd yell *I do not like green eggs and ham!* Then shrill laughter tinkling though windows like chimes or drapes in a summer breeze that remind you of clean things like hope and little girl bodies pulled wet and long from the tub.

I walked outside to see if Momma needed anything or if Hula wanted cheese on her hash browns, and Momma, the skin on her forehead lacy with veins the color of water at night, had her head tilted back, soaking up the summer sky hot on top of us, her smile smooth and sure, her necklace caught up in Little Hula's hair—Willie's hair—Little Hula cheek-smashed against Momma's breast, smiling the smile of girl dreams, the book open and dangling from her tiny hand, but held there. And Momma gone.

I thought of Fast Eddie, his philosophy about deciding the way and the when of how you go, of Momma putting her hand out and saying, No sir, not today, I've got reading to do with Little Hula here, and God listening.

Willie came back before Momma's mind left.

Of course he did, Momma said when I told her. They always do, one way or another.

Then she told me my father turned up on our doorstep the summer I turned nine. She peeled back the drapes and there he stood, his hat in is hand, in the same black suit, too short in the sleeves, he'd worn to weddings and funerals when they'd been together.

What did he have to say? I asked.

Don't know, she said. I didn't let him in.

All those years of her lost in the quiet of that room with *Employees Only* on the door. All those poems, desperate words about her body against his, not knowing where one began and the other ended.

Why? I asked.

You were asleep, she said. I didn't want to wake you.

Little Hula and me were at the post office sending off bills when I felt a hand on my shoulder. He looked the same. A few crinkles around the eyes, but still dangerously Willie.

Hi, I said. It was all that came to me.

He palmed Little Hula's dark head, like he should want to touch her but didn't. At three she already knew to dimple, was already a flirt.

She looks like me, he said.

Yeah, wouldn't you know it, I said.

What's her name?

Little Hula, I said.

I thought you were naming her Cheyenne, he said. I always liked the idea of that, Cheyenne.

I did, I said. But it didn't stick.

He handed me an envelope with an address in south Texas and a telephone number and two hundred dollars in it and drove off in his grandma's blue Chevy. I pointed the car out to Little Hula, told her in a few years I'd tell her a story about that Chevy, a story she should remember.

I tried calling a few months later, thinking Hula should know her daddy, thinking I should know her daddy, remembering his heat against my thigh, in my belly, but the line had been disconnected with no forwarding number.

Good Lord, Hula, my momma said, what did you expect?

Then she laughed, shooting spit though that beautiful piano-key gap.

PoJo's
and the
Buttery
Slope

PoJo's and Nelly's Buttery Nipples. You can't taste the butterscotch schnapps, and that's dangerous. Nelly loves serving Buttery Nipples because she's got herself a third nipple and it gives her a chance to brag about it to newcomers. Except for Will Saints, who dated Nelly the year before and swore he'd sucked on it as good as the other two, no one believed that nipple existed. Then last New Year's Nelly whipped her shirt up, yanked it over her lace bra, and right next to her left titty was an almost-titty, a little nubby nipple perky as anything.

We all got our tricks.

Mine's clasping my hands behind my back and pulling them over my head without unclasping them, which isn't nearly as sexy as a third nipple or putting both legs over my head like some girls can, but if a guy's already wanting to like me, it sometimes clinches the deal.

Youngblood wanted me but never liked the arm trick.

"Don't ever do that again," he said, leaning his short frame on the pool table over by the thumping PoJo's jukebox. "Didn't your momma teach you respect for the body?"

My momma taught me many things about a woman's body, but respect wasn't one of them.

"And who're you?" I said, already deciding that I liked the way his jeans hugged his thighs, the chain that winked from his wallet to his belt loop, that he kept his face shaved baby sweet. I'd been showing my trick to a life insurance salesman at the bar, hoping Youngblood would notice. When I saw him walk in, slanted cheekbones and a smirk like he knew something I wanted to know, I'd planned on ignoring him until he spoke to me. I knew he would.

"I'm yours," Youngblood said, and everyone in the bar groaned and rumbled and Nelly said a line like that deserved a shot and fixed me up a Buttery Nipple and Youngblood a Jack Daniels, and we toasted each other and drank. Then Youngblood smiled for the first time, dimples eating his cheeks, a gray front tooth that bent in a bit. I fell in love with that tooth before I fell in love with him.

We talked all night. I told him about my daddy who'd died the year before and my brother who talks to things that aren't there and about how Sam was born, me young and scared, him cut from me like a pit, my belly crisscrossed and scarred, how I sometimes think that's why he's so distant, because he didn't pass through the most intimate part of me like a baby should. How his daddy died on the job without Sam ever knowing him, and how it's hard to share him on account I was so young I barely know him to share.

And Youngblood offered his story, which was about the same but his.

I told him I wasn't one to pick up anybody in a bar.

He said he wasn't just anybody.

I didn't tell him I was engaged.

He didn't tell me he was married.

We went to the girls' bathroom because there's not as much

piss on the floor as the men's and made out against the mirror. He said he didn't mind my fat, or that I was pushing six feet. I told him I loved his gray, bent smile, the fact I could tuck his curly head under my armpit. I picked him up and set him on the sink and he laughed, giving up that tooth.

We both knew it was going to be bad.

After PoJo's, we went over to Nelly's place and she made us Western-style omelettes and strong coffee like shooters. Nelly said she lived in Europe once in her twenties and talked about how *in Europe* any chance she got. I lived in New Jersey once, I said, when my daddy sent me to my momma's for the summer and she hooked up with the steelworker. But somehow Jersey failed to be as exciting as Nelly's walk along the Riviera and her cheese nibbling with Jean or Paul. Although Nelly's my best friend, nights like that I hated her extra nipple and her blonde hair and her tiny waist and her Europe and the way she made an omelette without breaking it.

I ate everything, half of Nelly's too, then stared at my crumb-speckled plate like I'd just encountered it, barely remembering anything going down, still feeling empty and open and waiting.

After the omelettes, I gave Nelly fifty bucks to let us use her room. Since she didn't have company, she agreed.

I'd never done that before, although I'd do it again.

"You're beautiful, like one of those paintings," Youngblood said later, when we were naked, him pushing so far up my belly I thought I'd splinter gratefully, handfuls of me in his fists, a nipple under that gray tooth.

For the first time in years, I wasn't hungry.

PoJo's is what I do at night. Sam's what I do in the morning, before going to the lumberyard where I run the cash register and keep the books.

"You look like shit," he says every morning, dark eyes and darker mood, his booted feet slamming down the stairs and out the door. Sam was a colicky baby, red faced and wailing. It never got any better. Most days he wears one of his daddy's faded work shirts, the shirttails flapping at his knees. He didn't get my height and pretends it doesn't bother him. I try to be up before school because I think it's important to have him a hot meal, although I usually end up eating it. I don't remember when he started talking that way.

I sometimes hate my son.

Sam's turned me into his counselor twice for staying out all night. I had to go up to the school and talk to the lady, a woman fatter than me, her hair sprayed into a helmet, her lips razor thin and carved from her chin with fuchsia lipstick.

Sam has resentments, the woman says. Issues about his father. Issues about your drinking.

I said, Sam's fifteen, older than I was when I had him. That I stayed out because I didn't need to be driving, and wasn't that more responsible? That I made him breakfast every morning and he wouldn't eat it. That I had issues about his daddy dying, too.

She patted my hand, shuffled some papers, made a few notes, and said we should make an appointment to meet with her together, but didn't set up a date before I left.

Later at PoJo's, I told Nelly about Sam, about the counselor, about how I wasn't staying out anymore, how I was going to clean up my act. I stayed on the wagon that night. Had two Sprites and a Roy Rogers and felt clean for it.

"You're doing good," Nelly said when she fixed my Roy Rogers, putting in extra cherries as a treat. "Do what you got to do to keep your boy."

Nelly's girl Michelle lives with her daddy because Nelly got stoned one January afternoon and drove to the grocery to buy dinner and left Michelle in the carseat and lost track of time. A cop patrolling the parking lot found the girl huddled crying in the backseat, no jacket, no shoes. On her thirteenth birthday Nelly sent Michelle a makeup set in pink pastels, one like she'd wanted as a girl, and a gold locket that cost her two weeks' tips. It took everyone at PoJo's over an hour to decide which card to send and what to put in it. I thought she should write a poem. Annie thought that would disgust a kid. We finally settled on a card with a woman holding a little girl, roses floating in the background. Nelly wrote inside in a careful script, *If I can't be your mother, I would love to be your friend.* The presents and card were returned.

"What harm would it have done," Nelly said, me holding one

hand and old Annie holding the other, "letting her have them presents. I couldn't hurt her none from all the way across state."

"The problem," Annie said, "is that kids today don't know how good they've got it." Annie Willis is not a young woman, nor an attractive one, and you can tell youth didn't treat her any better.

"I know," said Nelly. "How many mothers in my situation would even bother trying? You ought to get something for trying."

"Shit," said Annie, "Fred tries, and he don't ever see his girls. Their mother refuses to bring them. But he still writes them, every week. Now that's a daddy. May not be the one they want, but at least he wants them."

The Fred and Annie thing keeps the town talking. Fred's in the pen for three counts of auto theft, and since he's past sixty, probably won't be seeing this side of the bars again. Annie got his name and address through some organization that matches up lonely women with lonelier prisoners. When Annie gets drunk enough she reads some of his letters and poems, the dirtier parts edited out, and afterward she toasts him, wishing he was here, and we all raise our glasses and cheer. Then Annie cries without making noise until her gray head sinks to the bar and we have to drag her to Nelly's to sleep.

Annie says she's got it better than most women. At least she knows where her man is.

When Annie's not around, Nelly says things could be worse. She could be Annie.

———————

I sometimes wonder where Joe is now, if there's a heaven and what it's made of, what he does all day, if there are days in heaven. Usually I just think of him as gone.

I met Joe when I was fourteen, walking to the store to fill the gas can for my daddy's mower. He drove by in his Ford, the old kind that peels down to a dull gray. He slowed when he saw me, whistled, tipped his hat, said, "Good Lord, you're killing me."

At fourteen I was at that age where you never leave the house without being lipstick smeared and hair sprayed, every turn of the corner a possibility. I ignored him but pushed my chest and butt out, glad I hadn't worn a bra.

"Them things are weapons," he said, impressed. "Shoot straight to the heart." He clutched at his chest. My eyes never left the horizon.

I wouldn't get in the truck, but he rode beside me, sweet-talking the whole way. At the station he paid for the gas and filled the can for me, threw it in the bed of his truck, told me I didn't have a choice now if I wanted the gas, and took me back to my place. We didn't talk, just listened to old crackling music on the AM station and let summer wrap itself around us. He had a tattoo of a spider on his right forearm and it shimmied across the web of his veins when he turned the wheel.

I never had a choice.

The next afternoon and every afternoon after he turned up on my front porch. My daddy scowled but didn't say a word. I had a good daddy. He appreciated that kind of need.

Joe was twenty-one, skin tanned to thick, his body well used, full of a jittery energy that would quiet only when he found his way into me. He told me once, after we'd made love on the bed of his truck in the mouth of July, that I reminded him of one of those radio contests where you call in at the right time with the right answer and win a key and if your key unlocks the car it's yours. Said he'd finally got his timing right, finally found the girl who he was made to unlock, which sent fire down my spine, wondering how many girls he'd tried before me.

He asked me to marry him the day before I was supposed to start tenth grade. Took me for a walk through the dying yellow of late summer up to Beacon Road where he first saw me. He'd spray-painted in red BELLE DILLON OWNS ME, SO I MIGHT AS WELL SIGN MYSELF OVER. WILL YOU MARRY ME?

Within two months I was pregnant. Within three he'd sliced himself open with a cord used to bind lumber. It snapped off when he was unloading it, snaked around his throat razor edged and dropped him dying. He bled to death on-site. I sometimes collapse those two events, him asking me to marry him and his bleeding death into the ground, the red spray paint and the red of the blood tying the two incidents into one memory of loss.

Owning a man, I learned, usually means you're empty handed.

After the second counselor incident, I wouldn't sleep over at Nelly's when Youngblood came through town every other week on his sales route. Instead, I'd get up right before the sun and sneak back to my place, just a few blocks away, and smoke cigarettes and sip coffee and imagine Youngblood with his wife, who I knew was a tiny redhead because I'd asked. I saw his fingers, strangely long and graceful for such a short man, picking their way over her bony ribs, his penis soft and finished and familiar against her skinny thigh, that gray tooth nibbling on her girlish nipple as an afterthought. Later, their daughters would climb into bed, maybe complaining of a bad dream, and he might sing to them like he sang to me when I woke from crying in my sleep, warbled songs about roads leading to places he would never take me.

Sleeping with Phil made it worse.

Phil's what I do for Sam and my brother Leonard. We've been engaged for four years but still live apart. We've discussed moving in together but never finish the discussions. He owns the Wooden Nickel, the nicest bar in town, which isn't exactly a compliment. He has to work there late most nights, so he's relatively low maintenance. I tell him I hang out at PoJo's so he doesn't think I don't trust him, so I don't crowd his space. He tells me I'm an independent woman. If he knows or thinks differently he doesn't care enough to mention it.

"Do you love me?" I ask Phil some nights, wondering what kind of man would let his woman run all over town, what kind of woman I am to be with a man who would.

"I've had love," Phil says. "This works better."

Phil's pushing sixty and quiet for it. He never asks for more than dinner and occasional sex, nothing kinky, straight-up missionary, a blow job thrown in now and again. We watch TV and play poker, talk about movie stars and magazines. Occasionally we dress up and go to Picasso's for a nice dinner and a bottle of wine and he tells me I'm pretty, opens the car door.

Some nights when I wake up crying he's staring at me, brown eyes like mud, his doughy body spilling white in the night.

"Is this enough?" I ask him.

"Trust me," he says. "Any more'd kill me."

Phil sleeps with his own sadness.

But he owns the Wooden Nickel, and in exchange for what I give him, the lack of responsibility somehow making it harder, he gives me money for Sam and pays for Leonard's boarding and doctors' bills and police fines, which aren't cheap.

Ninety percent of the time my baby brother Leonard's like any other man in town. He gets up in the morning, bags at the Piggly Wiggly, eats dinner sometimes with me, sometimes at old Annie's where he boards. Leonard's a handsome man. Looks like my daddy, tall and weedy, sucked-in cheeks and shadowed eyes tilted up toward his temples, hair wiry like exclamation points. He's had tons of girls, but they all eventually leave.

He paints oils, slicked colors that shouldn't go together but do. Reds licking into greens. Oranges blended to purple. Never anything definite like a house, or a prairie, or a seashore, just suggestions. But you always feel you're looking at something, something just out of your reach, something you should know but you don't, and you're somehow poorer for missing it. It's hard being near beauty like his.

Every now and then I get a call from the station that Leonard's being Leonard. Flashing the girls at cheerleading practice. Howling naked from his roof. Harassing people with dirty limericks in the park. About once a year I get a call that he's out in the high school football field naked, his paintings a mess of piss and gasoline burning, him dancing and wailing, throwing himself into the flames, then jumping back out, wishing he could do it. When new women meet him they always ask about his burn scars, tell him they're sexy. He says he got them from a plane crash and they believe him when they want to.

I saved one painting. I call it "The Flower" because the pinks and the reds and the creams stretch into strings of green and I'm the kind of person who needs a name for things.

For a while every time he came for dinner he'd try to steal it, just whip it off the wall and shove it under his coat, but I caught him at the door and refused to drive him home till he gave it back. Finally Phil anchored it to the wall, hammered straight through it, the paint singeing around the heads of the nails.

Sometimes Leonard stares at it and cries, his hands shoved to fists in his pockets, his body rocking back on his heels, says "Why are you doing this to me Belle? Why do you hate me?" Most times he won't look at it at all.

"Do you think I'm a whore?" I asked Nelly one night near Christmas when I was still seeing Youngblood. PoJo's was strung with lights, some of them blinking, some not. A Santa that used to dance a jig to "Here Comes Santa Claus" perched in the corner but wouldn't dance anymore since some drunk threw it at the jukebox.

"What for?" Nelly said. "Because of you and Youngblood?"

"Naw," I said. "For doing what I do with Phil."

"Shit," said Annie, already plastered. "You ain't whoring, just being practical."

At the time Fred's letters to Annie had quit coming, and she'd been on a streak.

"Well ain't that what whoring is?" Nelly said, winking.

"Youngblood doesn't like it," I said. "Says it ain't right, the way me and Phil are."

Actually, Youngblood hated it, said I wasn't respecting myself, said I was trading my body for money, said this naked, his short legs pumping around Nelly's bedroom, his lips screwed into a fist, his dick in a tight angry curl.

"And you're treating me better?" I said. "Keeping me on the side?"

He walked over and ripped off the blanket I always kept wrapped around me after making love. He knew this hurt me most, my flesh open, my fat drooping defeated around me.

"Is that what you think?" he asked, looking me up and down.

He punched a hole through Nelly's wall.

I had to tell her we were overzealous, that it was an accident. She'd sighed, said she was jealous.

"Don't like it?" Annie said, barely holding on to our conversation. "Ain't right?" She fished around in her purse and pulled out a piece a paper that had been ripped up, then taped back together. "I'll tell you what ain't right. What ain't right is a man writing this to a woman, and then a week later quit answering her letters. That's what ain't right."

Did I mention
that I love you
like the white part
of the breast against the bone
before you know
people are exploited
to debone it?
I wish I could bone you soon.
Did I mention,
I miss you
like I missed Santa and Jesus
when I was told
they didn't exist?
Did I mention
that you
are the me I forgot
to know
until I met
me in you?

Annie slurred through most of it, repeating lines, the syllables
jerking out of her mouth in soft clumps. "It's called 'Did I Mention,'" she said when she finished.

"Good God," Nelly said. I don't think she meant it kind.

"I know," said Annie, crying in her silent way, old and only
getting older and knowing it. "Can you believe they cage beauty
like that?"

Later Annie fell asleep on the bar, her cheek slack, her tongue
collapsed against her bottom lip. When me and Nelly picked her
up to take her back to Nelly's place, that poem fell on the floor,
and when Nelly wasn't looking, I slipped it into my jacket. It's the
meanest thing I've ever done. But I had a peculiar need to own
something, something that meant something to someone.

My last night with Youngblood I walked into PoJo's, him tweak-
ing Nelly's third nipple. She yanked her shirt down quick and he
winked his gray-toothed smile.

"Ain't that something," he said.

"It's something all right."

Nelly poured me a Buttery Nipple and a draft, then took off wiping down tables no one had used.

Later at Nelly's place I didn't want the omelette and the coffee. Instead I asked for a bottle. Nelly got out a pint of vodka and a hot-pink shot glass with the Eiffel Tower on it. The three of us sat on the floor Indian-style, playing quarters like high school. After a few rounds we forgot to play, me staring off, thinking about Youngblood touching Nelly, about Sam shrinking from my touch. Youngblood flipped the quarter in his fingers, trying to move it from his index finger and thumb to his ring finger and pinkie without dropping it. Nelly went to the kitchen to get ice cream.

She came back with a pint of Rocky Road, slumped to the couch, licking her spoon slow and twisting.

"Did you know," she said after a minute, "that one third of the ice cream sold is vanilla?" I thought she might cry. "Ain't that sad," she said. "All the choices in the world. You got your double fudge, your bubble gum, your chocolate, your mint, God knows how many you got, and one third picks vanilla."

"Let's go to bed," Youngblood said, rubbing my thigh.

"Maybe they like vanilla," I said, pouring myself another in the Eiffel Tower shot glass.

"There ain't nobody that really likes vanilla," Nelly said.

That night Youngblood couldn't get off. We tried for hours. Him on top, me on top, both sitting up, me on my belly, my ass heaving mounds. Finally, I slipped down his wiry frame, my fat suctioning to his sweaty skin, tugging me. He crossed his arms behind his head, linked one ankle over the other, watched. I took him in my mouth, his dick hard but soft, the kind of hard without purpose. My lips went numb trying, my neck tight and sore, spit pooling warm in the back of my throat, slicking down my chin.

Finally Youngblood pushed me off him, turned his back to me, yanked the comforter under his chin, leaving me the sheet.

"It ain't working," he said, his back a mess of asymmetrical tattoos. A big-tittied lady with swirling hair like water rode the base of his spine. A snake coiled on his shoulder blade. Random names and figures with stories he never told me.

"All I can see," he said, "is you with him, in the same way, naked with his dick in your mouth." I didn't know if this was true, or if he was just embarrassed about not being able to function, but either way, it was uncalled for.

"And you don't sleep with your wife?" I said, my voice shriller than I meant.

"That's different," he said. "We're married. I'm obligated."

I couldn't remember the last time we'd talked about him leaving her.

"Screw you," I said.

He snorted.

I fell asleep trying to miss Joe, trying to remember being someone's wife, my hands folded like prayer between my thighs, our bodies not touching.

I woke to a light tapping on the door. It was past four. I hadn't meant to stay so long. When I opened the door Nelly stood there, eyes ringed with smeared mascara, crust in the corners of her mouth. She had on an oriental silk robe that gaped open, showing the edge of her third nipple. In the darkness it looked more like a lumpy mole than a nipple.

"Sorry to bother you," she whispered, "but Sam's at the door."

I wrapped a comforter around me, spit on the corner of it and wiped under my eyes, then headed for the front door.

Sam stood in the open doorway, his arms crossed, a wool cap cutting across his forehead making his dark eyes overly apparent, his shirttails flapping against his skinny thighs. Sam has his daddy's eyes, knowing eyes, and it hurt me to look in them, to see him knowing me. My pudgy arms billowing over the comforter. My hair matted with hair spray and liquor and sex. My eyes bloodshot, the tender skin around them purpled and lined. I tried to keep a hand over my mouth so he couldn't smell the night I'd had.

"It's Uncle Leonard," Sam said. "He's having his bonfire down at the high school."

Phil's Honda Accord idled at the curb. I could see him flipping stations, blowing in his hands and rubbing them together against the cold. He never looked up at Nelly's.

"Give me a minute," I said. Sam nodded, stood there not moving, just staring at me. He looked like an old man, tiny and brittle and unyielding.

On the way back to the bedroom I passed Nelly sitting on the living room couch, fingering the Eiffel Tower shot glass.

"Everything okay?" she said, not looking up.

"Just Leonard," I said.

"Belle," she said, balancing the shot glass on her index finger, where it wobbled but stayed, "you know what?"

"What?" I snipped, not in the mood for a revelation or an insight into life.

"I got this shot glass at a thrift store," she said, setting it on the coffee table, still staring at it. "I ain't ever been to Europe."

"Who has?" I said.

When I got back to Nelly's room, Youngblood was sitting Indian-style in bed, arms crossed around his chest, his biceps bulging ropy.

"You're going to him," he said.

"It's my brother," I said. "This has nothing to do with Phil."

"Then why's he outside? I see a man in the car."

Part of me hoped Phil hadn't seen Youngblood seeing him. Part of me hoped he had. Either way, I suspected nothing would have changed.

"There's no time for this," I said, dropping the comforter, pulling up my panties, shoving my bra in my purse. "My brother's torching himself up at the school."

Youngblood walked over, grabbed me by the arm, whipped me onto the bed, straddled my hips, his knees biting into my soft flesh. I might be almost twice his size, but I will never know his anger. I didn't even try to buck him.

"Don't go to him, Belle," he said, tracing his finger along the C-section scar on my belly, the faded tracks where they took Sam from me.

I didn't answer. I didn't know what he was asking.

"Please, Belle," he said, his hands kneading my belly. "We can make this right."

I turned my head away from him.

Almost casually, like liquid pouring, Youngblood delved his fist into my abdomen. My breath lurched. He laid his head on my breasts, his knees and elbows drawn tight around me, his mouth whispering warmth against my skin.

My hands wouldn't take him. My arms sagged weighted at my side.

"You're never going to let anybody in, are you?" he said after a minute, sitting up.

I leaned forward, eased his lips apart, pressed my finger against his bent tooth.

When I left he was standing in the window, the drapes drawn open to the street, a cigarette between his lips, the smoke sifting down on him in thin, gray layers.

I walked to the Accord, exhaust coughing into the cold night, Sam and Phil hunched statues in the front, their faces waxen. They weren't looking at each other. They weren't watching for me.

Tammy, Imagined

Sometimes Tammy would overhear a person her grandparents' age say bitterly, "No one cares about anything anymore," and Tammy would picture herself in a few years, standing in a street of a town where she had never been, a place where she was of great importance, a banner wrapped over squared shoulders, arms raised in fury, protesting something of significance, a crowd of followers in similar poses marching behind her. There would be microphones shoved in her face and a voice cutting through the low rumble asking, *Ms. Wynbrite, how do you feel about the President's response to your organization's demands?*

Tammy's breasts would heave, her thin forearms quiver like stalks of wheat in a storm. She was a storm. Her voice a gale-force wind. And the Tammy sitting in her kitchen doing homework, ignored by her parents, or the Tammy slurping chocolate milk in the Midland High Cafeteria, ignored by her classmates, decided that the Tammy with WE HAVE VOICES, TOO scrawled across her rounded breasts, the Tammy who had seen the world, the Tammy the world had seen, would raise a fist, a fist mirrored by the gaggle behind her, and say "Response? There has been no response! He shall hear the roar of his own silence!" And then her group roars, or something to that effect.

Only Tammy was in the tenth grade, and so her revolutionary activities consisted of watching her father, who owned the only car dealership in town, make an affair of handing out twenties to the less fortunate looking people loitering downtown after the Wynbrite family attended church at Midland's Willing Baptist. Dressed in his sharp, pinstriped suit, his Rolex flashing, his face loosening into middle age, he'd peel crisp twenties off a big roll and place the bills into each palm with a handshake and a respectful nod.

"Charity," he'd say to Tammy on the ride home, "starts in your own backyard."

"So does crack smoking," Mrs. Wynbrite would advise, looking strangely adolescent in one of her new floral dresses from the juniors' department, sure the recipients of her husband's generosity would smoke, snort, or shoot the money. "My Henry," she'd sigh, stroking his thigh like a spaniel, "his heart's just greater than his good sense."

If anyone ever pointed out Mr. Wynbrite's Christian generosity, perhaps hinting at wilder stories from his younger days, he'd laugh, shrug his big shoulders, smile his sales smile, and say, "I was a boy then. I tell you, I'm a changed man. A changed man."

When Mrs. Zinner, Tammy's tenth-grade biology teacher—a tall woman with hands so wide she could palm her prized two-liter jar of wormed-through dog hearts with ease to spare, and skin so pale Tammy spent many hours trying not to trace the map of veins on her arms and calves—spoke to their class of Darwin and evolution, Tammy always pictured her father morphing from the primitive Neanderthal her mother swore he once was into the slicked-hair, slicked-smile salesman he'd become.

Evolution: the promise of change.

Like most teachers at the understaffed Midland High, Mrs. Zinner doubled as something else. She was the girls' basketball coach and the faculty advisor for the Young Humanitarians Club, where she arrived at the early November meeting waving a newspaper and vowing that United States soldiers needed their help. Mrs. Zinner read them an article by Dear Abby, who was concerned for the soldiers overseas, many of whom would not receive presents or mail at Christmas. This seemed a travesty to Mrs. Zinner, young boys forgotten in foreign lands.

When Tammy got home from school that afternoon she went to her father's study and took a stack of his thick yellow stationery with a silver looped "W" on the flap, an ornate design that seemed exotic. She spread out her stationery on the kitchen bar where her mother was cleaning a chicken for dinner. Mrs. Wynbrite had just started throwing around the word menopause in the same manner Tammy's father threw around the word communism, both words indicating a threat against the Wynbrite way of living.

"I tell you," her mother said, her hand up the backside of the chicken, "from now on I'm buying the boneless kind. Thirty years of cleaning chickens. I deserve boneless breasts."

It did not escape Tammy that boneless breasts were a metaphor for many things her mother thought she deserved.

Mrs. Wynbrite deserved a maid who did things like stick her own hand down the bowl of a toilet or up the backside of a chicken. She deserved the three children she lost through miscarriages, at least one of whom would have liked her. She deserved a husband who understood just how hot her body burned. Just how cold her body flashed. Just how oppressive her anxiety attacks were, sometimes causing her to pull off the side of the rode to hyperventilate. She deserved a house in Gulf Shores instead of the timeshare with the bad wicker furniture they rented two weeks out of the year, a week of which she spent alone with Tammy because Henry wouldn't leave the dealership. She deserved a daughter who liked pretty bras with bows in the center, who wanted to be taught the art of makeup and flirting, who would wear a dress that showed off her figure, which, as Mrs. Wynbrite well knew, wouldn't last forever. And most of all, she deserved a family who understood how hard it was for a beautiful woman to come to terms with the fact she was no longer beautiful while suffering hot flashes in a kitchen with her hand up the backside of a chicken.

"You know," Mrs. Wynbrite said, collapsing on a stool beside her daughter, the chicken squatting, still in its skin, on a plate on the bar, "they never tell you going through menopause makes you feel less than a woman."

Outside the sun dipped into the horizon. A leaf spun in the sunlight, brushing against the kitchen window. The fading light softened her mother's face, made her seem accessible, a place Tammy could visit and feel at home.

Mrs. Wynbrite tugged the skin at her temples tight, trying to pull her crow's-feet smooth, her rusty rouged cheeks stretching into her hairline. Someone, somewhere, had told Mrs. Wynbrite that her color scheme was autumn, and ever since then her face had been painted in the colors of October, her hair a peculiar shade of dying leaves. She pulled a mirror from her purse and experimented, yanking her skin in different directions. She looked like her teeth and eyes were going to pop from her skull.

"Think I should get a few tucks?" she said, winking, her fingers at her temples prohibiting her from closing her eyes entirely.

Tammy knew better than to answer.

Mrs. Wynbrite put down the mirror, pushed Tammy's hair from her eyes, a familiar action that prompted Tammy to grow it even longer. She stared at Tammy's face, brushing her knuckles against Tammy's jawline, across her lips, under her eyes.

She dropped her hand from Tammy's face, sighed like she was giving something up. Her breath smelled of the celery she had chopped for dinner, the slight scent of whiskey.

"You should have seen me," she said, smoothing her apron over her thighs. "I really was something else."

There were pictures in photo albums of Mrs. Wynbrite, her legs thin and willowy, lips dark and plump, young men handing her corsages. Her face sure of what was to come.

"Less attractive women, they learn to manage at a young age. But beautiful women. Beautiful women are cursed with charmed lives until they're fifty and then *poof!*" Mrs. Wynbrite snapped her fingers. "Their insides dry up and their husbands ignore them and the gas attendants and cashiers and men passing on the street look through them like they're not even there."

Tammy saw a tundra, skulls scattered around, much like the exaggerated, desolate plains in movies about prehistoric times. Mrs. Wynbrite, her face tucked almost away, teeth square and protruding like wooden shingles, eyes buggy, stumbled over the thin-soiled ground, thirsty, her body promising to offer up dust. Stretched before her was the cavernous ruin of a female body, the rib cage smoldering white, spiky fern fingers reaching up empty-handed. *Wait!* Mrs. Wynbrite might scream, tumbling to her knees, *I am this carcass!* Much wailing.

"Do you understand what I'm saying?" Mrs. Wynbrite asked, stroking Tammy's cheek. "Men want one thing, and then you're old, and they don't even want that anymore. No one told me this when I was your age."

"Dad thinks you're beautiful," Tammy said, thinking this should be enough.

Her mother arched a brow, stared at Tammy with shaded eyes, eyes that said *You'll get yours soon enough.* She rose, picked up the chicken, and went to the sink, turning her back on Tammy.

"Your father doesn't think I'm beautiful," she said. " He doesn't have to anymore."

Tammy never intended for what happened to happen. She started writing her first letter.

Dear Soldier,

My name is Tammy Wynbrite. I am a sophomore at Midland High in Midland, Alabama. My favorite subjects are sociology and English, although my school is rather poor and we don't have the best teachers and my fellow students are drunken idiots and so I don't have any friends and I wish I could take foreign languages but they don't offer any in my sucky school. I read in Dear Abby that you might not get any mail over Christmas, and it broke my heart, as your sacrifices for this country surely go unappreciated. My grandfather fought in WWII and when he died they give us a flag and we raise it on Veteran's Day and the Fourth of July and Memorial Day and never leave it up after dark. Just so you know what kind of people we are.

Although I am not a believer in organized religion, as I disagree with many of the policies of the various institutions, I do find spirituality to be an important thing in life, and Christmas is as good a day as any to celebrate our love for each other. Besides, it must be hard to deal with childhood holiday memories when you are in such a strange land.

I hope to travel some, maybe with the Peace Corps, when I graduate from college, where I intend to study political science and philosophy. My hometown does not offer much culture (although my high school put on Romeo and Juliet last year and I played Juliet's maid) beyond racing around the Hardee's parking lot and the annual beauty ball, which is rigged for the principal's daughter (who's already had one kid) to win.

Anyway, I would love to hear about all of your travels. And I get lonely for other worldly people in this town. Please feel free to write me back.

Merry Christmas,

Tammy Wynbrite

Tammy read it aloud, fleshing out the girl the soldiers would imagine while reading her letter. Young. Maybe in braces. From small-town Alabama. Perhaps vulgar. Screaming things like *fuck you, asshole* across the high school parking lot in that nasal voice of girls who live on the edge of town with grandmothers the age of Tammy's mother. Payless shoes. A banana clip holding back her permed, poofed hair. Silvery blue eyeliner spreading her lids wide. Pleated jeans tapering into narrow tubes stopping high on the ankles, where her hair follicles would make her skin look big pored and clogged.

She could hear her mother weeping and hiccuping down the hall, which would go well into the night, long after they'd eaten their TV dinners in separate rooms. Suddenly, the prospect of sitting in a daffodil yellow kitchen in Midland, Alabama, with a half-skinned chicken and hair a strange shade of autumn leaves with nothing more to examine than the lines on her face seemed an inevitable, unbearable destiny.

She thought of the soldiers she saw on the army commercials on TV. Hair cut so short it glowed on the ends like one of those funky spidery lamps from the seventies. Smiles sharp and sure.

Their feet planted in the deserts of the Middle East. The jungles of Asia. Her life would be ruined if one did not write her back.

She rummaged through her dresser drawers until she found the package of pictures her mother had forced her to take at Glamour Shots the summer before. She looked at least twenty-one. Breasts pushed up from the underwire bra. Lips lined and glossed. Eyes kohled. Eyebrows plucked and arched. Brow bone highlighted in cream eye shadow. Cheekbones in pale pink. She had to admit, the woman in the picture, who she couldn't even connect to herself, looked damned good, if one liked that kind of woman.

Dear Soldier,
    My name is Tammy Wynbrite. I am a twenty-one-year-old dancer at the Thirsty Kitty in Midland, Alabama. I am currently dancing to put myself through school, where I am studying to become a poet. I got married directly out of high school to a man who preferred fists to words . . .

Dear Soldier,
    My name is Tammy Wynbrite. I am a twenty-one-year-old student at the local community college. I teach Sunday school at Willing Baptist, where I also play the piano. Both of my parents died in a car wreck when I was ten, and so I have learned to appreciate the guidance of our Heavenly Father . . .

Dear Soldier,
    My name is Tammy Wynbrite. I am a twenty-one-year old woman from Midland, Alabama, where I cashier at the local Pig. After reading about your loneliness in foreign lands, I knew that you would understand how alone I feel in this world. Sometimes I don't feel as if I can go on. The endless groceries. The string of men. No one listening to what I say. And then I read about brave men such as yourself, so many miles from home, and I think, Tammy Wynbrite, you're the most selfish woman on the face of the earth. Your faith and dedication help me . . .

She wrote ten letters, each woman tragic and complex, offering a cry that no man, especially a good-hearted soldier, could refuse. She sprayed them all with Jasmine Breeze, which made the ink run and blotch as if they'd been cried over, paper-clipped a glamour shot to the front of each letter, and walked them straight down to the mailbox, even though the mail wouldn't come until the next day.

On the way back into the house she passed her father consoling her mother, his tie loosened, his eyes tired, his hand anchored on her mother's shoulder as if she might drift away if he let her go, or as if maybe he would.

A few days after the New Year, the afternoon of Tammy's sixteenth birthday, Mrs. Wynbrite came home from shopping with thick, grayish tracks tracing the faint lines of where her almost invisible eyelashes sprouted. Her eyes were red and tender, the skin puffy. She looked liked she'd been in a fistfight.

"Surprise!" she yelled, shoving her face into Tammy's.

"Don't ever say your mother's not a rebel. I got my eyeliner tattooed on!" She twirled in a circle, then stopped, one hand gripping her cocked hip, the other splayed under her chin. She had on one of the black miniskirts she'd bought for Tammy, and it bunched around the hips, several sizes too small.

Two hours later, already late for their reservations at Tammy's favorite restaurant, the Southwestern Wind, where they served chili in a bowl made from bread, her parents were still in their bedroom, their voices unusually loud, splintering like broken glass down the hallway.

"This is not your day for once. It's your daughter's sixteenth birthday."

"When is it my day? It's never my day. I've never had a day. Not once. My funeral will be my day."

"You look like a fool. You paid good money for that?"

Tammy turned up the news—black boy soldiers, barefoot, gesticulating around camouflaged trucks. One had on a Coca-Cola T-shirt.

Tammy saw herself, slender and muscled, standing defiantly in the dusty deserts somewhere in Africa, young ebony men with regal bone structure hopping around her, waving guns like college students wave drinks at Mardi Gras. No one dressed in American propaganda.

An interviewer asked her, "Why are you here, Ms. Wynbrite? Why put your life in danger?"

Tammy, her voice righteous, replied, "Because these people look different than us, we abandon them, leave them to starvation and disease. If the French were starving and warring and dying, would we turn a deaf ear to their cause?"

The men behind her cheered her power and beauty, chanted her name in their language, a language Tammy, in her imaginings, understood intuitively.

After an hour, her parents emerged from their bedroom. Her mother had never looked worse. Trounced. Her father weary.

"How's the birthday girl?" he said, hugging her briefly. Lately, he'd become terrified of touching her, scared of her woman body, which neither of them knew what to do with.

Sometimes Tammy would stand naked in her bedroom, pinch the fatty place at the vortex of her thighs, suck in her belly, lean heavy on her dresser, her biceps tight against her rib cage, her breasts pressed into a deep crease. *Hello, Soldier*, she'd whisper as huskily as her girlish voice allowed, and she thought of taking up smoking, if only to acquire that raspy, Southern voice all the faster girls rolled off their glossy, twisting tongues.

"She's fine," Tammy said, shoving her hands to fists in the pockets of her baggy jeans.

"You're wearing that?" her mother asked, eyes permanently startled.

At dinner her mother got drunk. Called the waiter Juan even though he was Scotts/Irish from Montgomery. Told him he was a dashing young man. Asked for his number for her birthday girl. Tripped on the way to the bathroom. Sent back her meal twice. Insisted that the wait staff sing "Happy Birthday" in Spanish, during which she Oléd! and clapped with abandon.

When they got back home, her mother pitched herself up the red brick front steps, past the plastic azaleas resembling hair plugs in their suburban lawn, which she'd ceremoniously implanted last spring, refusing to tend to things anymore that insisted on dying. Her father took Tammy to the garage, where he kissed her on the cheek and handed her a set of keys.

"Happy Birthday, Sweetheart," he said. "Your mother picked it out herself." Inside there was a silvery blue Trans-Am with an orange pinstripe skunked down its sides. The lights flipped up like eyes. The back had a tail.

Tammy unlocked the driver's side door. Slid into the gray seat. Placed her hands in the 10-2 position like she was taught in Driver's Ed. Put her foot over the accelerator and slammed it hard.

She could already hear the comments in the Midland High parking lot. *Cool ride. Fucking nice wheels. Bad Ass.* Everything she never wanted. A redneck car.

Tammy pictured herself sitting in a garage on her sixteenth birthday in a used Trans-Am crying. Perhaps she would wait for her father to leave and turn on the ignition. Shut the garage door. Find a Velvet Underground tune on the radio. Roll down the window. Headline: Suburban teenager emotionally abused by parents commits suicide in her garage with birthday present. Caption under her glamour shots picture: "She didn't even leave a note, a good-bye. Nothing. Nothing to explain her pain," said Mrs. Wynbrite.

Tammy named her car Rebel, hung hot pink dice from the rearview mirror, put a half-naked Hawaiian girl on the dashboard, reasoning that if she was going to look country, she might as well do it right. She took to driving on backwoods roads after school. Past lazy cows with muddled, confused eyes that reminded her of her mother. Past rust-colored shacks with even rustier, jacked-up, tireless cars in the yards.

On certain stretches, the trees reached over Tammy in a canopy, the sun fingering through in a way that made her feel close to God, as if he were promising her better things to come. The tips of the late winter grass glowed orange in the afternoon sun, in the same way the soldiers' hair glowed in the army commercials, like the world was tipped in fire. She sang out loud to the songs on the radio and saw herself doing it while she did it.

She found an old abandoned filling station, one of the many fossils of a more prosperous time in their town. The door was unlocked, the counters and walls and floor spray-painted with anarchy symbols and rebel flags and who loves who and who's been where. In a back corner she found old boxes of orange nylons and makeup manufactured by a company Tammy didn't recognize, and she wondered if someone else's mother went half-mad during menopause and this was what was left of her. Tammy would pull a beach towel from the trunk of her car, spread it on the concrete floor of the gas station, take out her schoolbooks, and finish her literature, Spanish, biology, and algebra homework.

Problem: If one intelligent girl, age 16, currently on Planet X, has a mother, age 51, and a father, age 52, who are from Planet Y, and the teenage girl has two years before she graduates from high school and four years of college, how long before she finds her homeland of Planet Z, and does such a place exist?

After she finished her homework, she'd open the driver's side door to the Trans-Am (despite her father's warnings about running down the battery), pop in an Otis Redding or Jimi Hendrix tape, and write letters and poetry to her soldiers in the voice of one of the many Tammy Wynbrites. She'd rummage through the boxes of cakey, dried-out makeup and find colors that reminded her of passion or love or loss—Pink Pucker, Fire Rouge, Sultry Silver—and then smear her letters and poems with makeup, sometimes in an attempt at an actual image, but usually just mixing colors to reflect what she was feeling, which she couldn't quite place in a physical form anyway. Bruised purple. Angry reds. Dull silvers, flat. If Jimi was playing she'd circle her mouth in a violent shade of thick lipstick and wait until he sang *'Scuse me while I kiss the sky*, where she'd press her own lipsticked lips along the margins.

The same afternoon she received her first response from a soldier stationed in Korea, her mother found one of her lip-blotted poems:

A single slash,
That's all that's required,
To end feelings,
That evil sired.
Born to live,
Condemned to die,
In a world of hatred,
You're living a lie.

"Do you want to burn with Hell's Angels?" her mother shrieked, waving the poem in front of her. "Do you?"

"The speaker's not necessarily me," Tammy said. "You don't understand poetry."

"What? Our daughter's channeling now, Henry. You see what happens when you spoil her like you do?"

If Tammy were watching this on a sitcom, the audience would have laughed that mechanical, clipped laugh.

"It's just a poem," Mr. Wynbrite said, unequipped to deal with a situation that couldn't be solved by throwing in power locks and windows for free.

"Would you listen to me?" Tammy said. She imagined herself stomping her feet, taking the poem and ripping it into little pieces in front of her mother's face, then blowing the scraps like amputated wings past her mother's coiffed head. The scene felt very distant, like she was scripting it as it occurred. This was how she felt lately. *I should be angry. I should be happy. I should smile now.*

She snatched the poem and shredded it, sprinkled it around her mother like confetti.

Her mother slapped her.

Tammy saw an aging woman, a graying man, both well dressed, staring at a girl in ripped jeans and a black sweater, all of them strangers, stranded in a daffodil yellow kitchen in Midland, Alabama.

I should cry now, she thought. But she didn't.

Dear Tammy—
    Your letter was passed to me through many hands that felt we have some common ground. I am also from a small town in the South and I understand how lonely it can be. You must keep faith that things will get better, as they always do . . .
Please write back—
Lt. Michael Williams

In creating ten women, Tammy hadn't considered that the soldiers would be responding to each woman's letter they had received, and in assuming that the woman existed and knew who she was, would not designate their responses to *Tammy the Stripper* or *Tammy the Teetotaler* or *Tammy the Poet*. Michael enclosed a picture of himself sitting under a tree, dressed in army garb, his hand shielding his eyes from the sun. He was skinny, flat nosed, and from what she could tell, decidedly unattractive. He also sounded like a bit of a country boy, a bible thumper, and Tammy knew enough of them already to last her a lifetime. She shoved his letter into her dresser drawer, as she did with the next three that came, unsure of how or who she should be in responding. And then:

Dear Tammy,
My name is Parker Kent. I am a 25-year-old pilot stationed in the Philippines. I could not help but to respond to your letter, as I detected a certain, familiar pathos in your voice that elicited an emotion in me I have not felt in some time. I understand the complexities of love, your heartache at being discarded by the men who have been privileged to have known you. It's obvious from your picture that you are a very beautiful woman, and sometimes men take advantage of such things. I have enclosed a poem I wrote last night after awakening from a dream in which an old lover visited me . . .

> She came to me, sheer light for flesh,
> Her body, white and wanting, floating,
> Above me, another promise,
> Unfulfilled . . .

The poem turned pornographic, albeit hidden in flowery language. Tammy thought she should be scared or angry at such a suggestive letter, but she felt strangely calm, in control, aroused that the thought of her could make a grown man's belly flop. She locked her bedroom door. Got out her dictionary: **pathos** n. [Gk= suffering] *a quality in an experience, narrative, literary work, etc. which arouses profound feelings of compassion or sorrow.*

No one had written to her in Greek before, and she could be sure that the letters exchanged between crushes at school never contained poetry about phantom lovers or words that had to be looked up. She had his picture, a bulky man, brawny, ropy, his hair golden, his eyes crinkled at the sides. He stood in front of a helicopter, his feet shoulder-width apart, his hand clutching a helmet. Tammy wrote the date on the back, drew a heart that embarrassed her around it, and stuck his picture under her mattress.

She spent the rest of the evening formulating a response. At first she'd decided to keep the details sketchy, since she didn't know to which letter he was responding. Then she decided the more complex Tammy Wynbrite was, the more interesting she would be to Parker, so she combined the ten Tammys.

Because of her parents' untimely death, she married too young to a man who abused her, her high school sweetheart, and she escaped his wrath by throwing herself into church. And when Jesus failed her, she ran away from her husband, hiding in the small town of Midland, where she studied poetry at the junior college and worked nights at the Thirsty Kitty. She added some steamy parts from the historical romances she hid in her closet: *I am a woman of dishonor. More than one man has licked my luscious lips, caressed my silken skin into trembling submission and shared a rapturous loving, my female flesh moist and hot. But I am a woman for one man, my heart truthful, my soul yearning for your cleansing touch.* . . . She sprayed the letter with Jasmine Breeze and addressed it in a careful, feminine script.

She undressed, stared at her body in the mirror, cupped her breasts in each hand, said *Hello, My Love* in a throaty voice. She lifted one leg, propped it onto the dresser as if it were a chair on the stage at the Thirsty Kitty. Her vagina, completely exposed, winked back pink and unfamiliar from the mirror. She lifted her arms in a dancing motion, her breasts flattening. She imagined herself dancing for Parker, him in dog tags and a muscle shirt, her twirling her Glamour Shots push-up bra overhead, mimicking the helicopter blades in his photo.

Two months went by.

Her father worked late.

Her mother cried in the kitchen.

Tammy staked out the mailbox.

In early March she received a letter postmarked in Albany, Georgia, Parker Kent's name in the return address. It was an invitation to a coming-home celebration BBQ with a hand-drawn map of how to get to the Kent farmhouse. He'd included another poem, this one raunchier than the last, and scrawled across the bottom, *It would mean the world to me if you'd come. Please.*

Tammy saw herself standing in front of the Kent farmhouse, red lipstick and powder pale, her hair a tight chignon. "I have dreams, responsibilities," she said. "I can't be a farmer's wife."

Parker, fighting tears, muscles bulging, holding her letters in his hand, said "I slept with these every night for two months, memorized your words, wrote you poetry in my dreams. We'll leave the farm. I don't need it. You're my home now."

A week before the picnic, Tammy went shopping. She bought a skimpy sundress—the fabric so sheer you could see her new thong and matching bra—and a slender pair of fire-red stiletto heels. On the way home she stopped at the gas station and purchased a map.

She slipped past her mother, who was sitting at the kitchen table paying bills, and went to her room where she changed into her new shoes and thong, then paraded around the room, tripping at first, the unfamiliar heels catching in the thick carpet. She stopped in front of the mirror, her rear facing it, twisted her torso quickly, her hair whipping against her cheek, and bent at the waist, the pale, moon-shaped curve of flesh under her buttocks where the sun didn't touch disappearing as she straightened upright. Then she did it all over again.

After she perfected the move, she got out the map, squatted on the floor, and calculated the driving time to Albany. Four hours and twenty-five minutes. In colored pencils she traced the thin lines indicating the tiny roads which passed through the small dots of the small towns, assuredly just like hers, all the way to Albany. She made a violet line through Auburn, through Columbus, through Cussetta, through Weston, through Leesburg. She saw herself dressed in her sundress, driving through these dots, these towns, her window down, the sun teasing her hair, aware that people were gawking at her beauty. She was singing out loud, screaming really, as if she didn't see them seeing her, and them thinking how she was so wild and free she didn't care if she made a scene. She imagined her mother watching her go earlier that morning, standing in her bathrobe on their suburban two-car-wide sidewalk, gesticulating her arms wildly, screaming *Don't leave us*, her breasts spilling out in limp waves, Tammy feeling great empathy, but still driving on.

Only the morning of the BBQ, Mrs. Wynbrite refused to get out of bed, said why bother? Mr. Wynbrite responded by going to the dealership, even though he'd promised to take the day off. Tammy, dressed in her new outfit and full makeup, tripped right out the front door in her red stilettos and took off in her Trans-Am for Albany, Georgia.

This was the first trip Tammy had taken alone, and after she'd played her mixed tape three times, she began to get bored of the monotonous green of the countryside. She did have her window down, but the air was hot and moist and gritty and smelled like asphalt, so she closed it. When she came to a stoplight on a double-lane road, she made sure to exaggerate her mouth as she sang, so the drivers in the cars around her would notice how she didn't notice people looking at her. No one looked her way, except one kid in a beat-up Corvette who screamed *Cool fucking car* when he passed her on a double yellow line.

Around noon she exited 280 onto Jefferson Street into downtown Albany. At the entrance of the city there was a sign with "Quail Capital of the World" scrawled across the wing of a grinning bird. Albany looked just like Midland, but slightly bigger.

The Kent farm was exactly where the map indicated. A tiny white house with skinny trees stretching over it. A front porch painted a dull beige. A nondescript barn. The red dirt driveway was empty, and Tammy assumed she was the first to arrive.

She thought about how she should greet Parker. A handshake? Too formal. A hug? Somehow false. Welcome home? Maybe he would see her walking up, recognize her from the Glamour Shots photo, throw whatever he held in his hands to the ground, run to her, twirl her in a full 360-degree welcome-home movie circle.

They saw each other at the same time. Tammy with one freshly shaved and moisturized leg out the car door, him with a Silo cup in one hand and a sandwich in the other. He shoved the rest of the sandwich in his mouth and loped over.

"You made it," he said, wiping his mouth with the back of his hand. He was shorter than she imagined, about as tall as she was, and he had crow's-feet stretching toward his temples from squinting too much. She tried not to be disappointed.

"Of course," Tammy said in her throaty voice. She smiled what she hoped to be that kind of smile, although Parker didn't see it because he was talking to her breasts, which pleased Tammy in ways she couldn't explain.

"Do you need to go to the bathroom after being in the car so long?" Parker asked, and Tammy's mood clouded briefly, because although she wanted him to picture her in a compromising manner, that did not include squatting on a toilet.

"No," she said, sharper than she intended, and the conversation stumbled. They stared. They rocked on their heels. Tammy's dress stuck to her back. Her thong cut between her legs.

Finally Parker spoke, told her that everyone else would be there in an hour or so, and he'd introduce her to his father when he got back from buying meat at the grocery. He walked her around the farmhouse, which was just like every other farmhouse, quilts tossed over old furniture, tin pie pans hanging on the wall in the kitchen. He explained to her the various things he intended to do with the house over the summer, the porch he and his father were going to build, the new well they were going to dig, and Tammy tried to make clever comments, but since she'd never really done anything around the house besides cleaning her own room, could offer nothing more than, "Wow, that sounds really complicated," which made Parker talk louder and grin.

After the tour, he led her to the keg sitting in an army green trashcan behind the barn, where he filled her a cup of beer, allowing the foam to run over the top onto his hand. He handed her the beer, then put the tap directly in his mouth and drank for almost a full minute, beer streaking down his cheeks and onto his white T-shirt until she could see the pinkness of his nipples under the wet fabric.

"Hot damn," he said, "I miss the taste of beer made in America. Always tastes different overseas. The water or something."

He offered her the tap, and she wrapped her lips around it suggestively like she imagined Tammy Wynbrite from the Thirsty Kitty might do, let the bitter liquid roll down her throat until her head felt light on her shoulders. They traded the tap back and forth and after a half hour or so the blended lives of the many Tammy Wynbrites became difficult to keep in order, their details hard to recall. She couldn't remember if her parents had died when she was ten or twelve or how old she was when she married her husband or when she left him and if she worked at the grocery store while she was married to him or after she moved and how long she had danced at the Thirsty Kitty. But she pouted. Offered her cleavage.

Sighed. Sighed again. And said more than once, "Life's so much harder for a beautiful woman," her mother's voice slicing through her belly and riding off her tongue. Parker responded to almost everything with a "really fucking cool" or "that blows," then handed her the tap.

Tammy didn't realize Parker intended to kiss her until his tongue was in her mouth, one hand holding the nape of her neck, the other her hipbone. He kissed her hard, his tongue thick, tough like overcooked meat.

Tammy imagined herself sucking his tongue into her mouth, holding him there with her expertise, nibbling his flesh, the Tammy from the Thirsty Kitty taking over until he groaned and pushed himself against her.

Tammy didn't imagine biting him, but that's what she did, and the feel of his muscled tongue squeezed between her teeth sent fire to her belly, the taste of his blood mingling with beer and the salt of skin.

He jumped back, scared, clutching at his mouth. She grinned, snaked her tongue against air, spiked her heels in the ground.

"Are you okay?" Parker asked, looking at her strangely.

Tammy inched as close to him as she could without touching, only a seam of sunlight separating their bodies, heard herself whispering, "Are you going to do me or not?"

Parker jumped back again, looked around to see if there was anyone watching.

"People'll start getting here soon," he said.

"We'll hear them coming," Tammy said.

Parker didn't seem so sure. He walked over to a bench behind the barn and sat down, motioning for Tammy to come and sit beside him. Instead of sitting next to him, she artfully lifted one stiletto-tipped leg, like she'd practiced in her bedroom, and straddled him. He let his hands fall loosely to his sides so he wouldn't have to cup her buttocks. Tammy could feel him hard against her.

"Tammy," he said, still trying not to touch her, "I know you've been mistreated by men and all, but the guy's sort of supposed to initiate this kind of thing." He looked very sincere.

"How do you think up all those things you wrote me?" she said, rotating her hips. "Like pathos. How do you understand my pathos?"

Parker looked at his lap. Said, "I kind of had some help from my buddy. I didn't want you to think I was stupid, with you studying poetry and all."

Tammy felt a fist in her throat. She couldn't decide if it was anger or hurt. *I should be hurt now. Should be angry now. I should be what?*

Parker grabbed her hips, tried to lift her away from him. "I told you," he said, "the man is supposed to initiate all this."

"Why?"

"Because."

"Because why?"

"Because men are supposed to make the first move," he said.

"But what if they don't?"

Before Parker could answer, Tammy took him by surprise, had him flipped onto his back on the bench, still riding his hips. She made a sound, high and clear, a sound she didn't know her body was capable of producing, a sound like something afraid of dying. She twisted her hips until he moaned, pained, and when she leaned down to kiss him, her hair tumbling over her face and his, she didn't feel her stomach bubble up into her throat until she was already vomiting.

"Goddamn it, you crazy bitch," Parker yelled, pushing her off of him. He fell on one side of the bench, she on the other, her knees scraping against ground, her palms stuck in a mixture of soil and gravel and warm, regurgitated beer. They both crouched on all fours in the dirt, Tammy a mess of vomit and smeared red lipstick, Parker not faring much better. Tammy started heaving again, her belly straining, her eyes watering, her nose stinging, as if someone were holding her under water.

This is where, years later, Tammy's lovers would stop her in her story, perch up on their elbows, perhaps a hand cupping her bare breast, and say, "You've got to be kidding me. You really threw up on him?"

"I was something else when I was young," she'd say. "You should have seen me."

And she knew they did.

She had told the story this way, so many times, to so many lovers, that she could barely picture Parker, beer-drunk and indifferent, his tongue in her mouth, his hand reaching up her lovely sundress, groping. Her mother's voice: Men only want one thing and then one day you're old and they don't even want that anymore. Her stomach roiling from the beer until she ran to the farmhouse and threw up in the kitchen sink, right under a sampler with *Home Is Where The Heart Is* encircled by a thin cross-stitched heart. Parker standing in the doorway, lit by the sun behind him, still sipping beer out of a Silo cup, asking "How old are you really?" A look of disgust on his face. Boredom.

And instead of seeing herself running to her Trans-Am, tripping in her heels, Parker's laughter behind her, she could almost remember lifting herself off all fours behind the barn, wiping her mouth with the back of her hand, smoothing the skirt of her dress, tucking her hair behind her ears, maybe saying something witty and cutting like the high school boys at home who mixed Gatorade with vodka and puked out their car windows in the McDonald's drive-through with a *Can you Super-Size that?* Perhaps she did dance a Thirsty Kitty kind of dance back to her car, pausing at the car door to bend over and flash her thong, pouting playfully, saying *I'm sorry it didn't work out.* Surely she slipped behind the wheel of her Trans-Am, threw a waving hand out the window, her smile as broad and knowing as she could make it. And she started the ignition, waiting for the car to warm up as if she were in no hurry, knew of no such emotions as shame or want. Then she re-applied her lipstick in the rearview mirror and wiped the mascara from under her eyes before backing out of the gravel driveway, still waving, still smiling, until Parker was no more than a flesh-colored dot, like the dots on her map, indicating places Tammy had never seen, places that had never seen Tammy.

When You See

This I remember. It's the summer of my hot pink two-piece, the one with the tortoiseshell plastic circle at the breastbone. The summer of my Farrah Fawcett hairstyle, limp feathered wings against my cheeks, and I am bobbing up and down in the water, trying to keep my feet off the bottom of the lake, because I'm scared of things I can't see, and if you sit still I know the bream bite your freckles, although no one believes me.

My two cousins and my younger brother, all lanky, the beige color of sand and mutts and boys in summer, are skipping flat rocks from the shore, trying to hit me in the head. They rush the waves to dampen their trunks, pull the fabric away at their crotches to catch bubbles of air so their privates look huge and bulbous, then shimmy their hips in my face. They scream *Fatso*. They scream *Miss Piggy*. They've just realized that I've just realized my body. My biggest decision of the day will be whether or not to shave, worried that I might scrape off my new tan.

My mother ignores them. She floats in a Styrofoam chair, balancing a screwdriver on the armrest, her drink watery and thin, already melted in the summer heat. She's convinced that orange juice will help her tan, keeps pitchers of screwdrivers in the kitchen, and makes me run to the house—my bikini bottoms suctioning to my cheeks, my brown belly goose-bumped—to freshen her drink. She wears huge movie-star glasses that cover half her face, the lenses octagonal and burgundy. Her swimsuit is bumblebee-striped in pale pink and black, and dips in a V, showing off her breasts. Her legs, thin and white and freckled, press flat against the nylon webbing of the chair. She is everything I think a woman should be.

Our new house—three stories, sloped ceilings, brown brick—sits on a hill behind us, and we all steal glances now and again to see if it's really there, really ours, amazed that my father's last big deal, the real thing, was the real thing.

Occasionally I swim over to my mother and pull myself up using her armrest, water rushing over her, and she swats me gently, like a dragonfly, says go away.

My father, knobby kneed and pale in his khaki shorts, his belly a hard fist, straddles a riding lawn mower in a black cowboy hat. Every now and then he screams out "I wonder what the poor folks are doing?" and laughs at his own joke.

I am unbelievably happy.

"That's your happiest moment?" Robert asks. "More so than Europe even?"

We're sprawled naked across the bed in the master suite of what he calls his fishing cabin, although I know fishing cabins don't have master suites. The skin across my hipbone is stretched so thin it glistens. Robert's belly is taut and wiry like that of most middle-aged professors who realize they're middle-aged and work out religiously. His big toe rubs the arch of my foot, his right hand cupping my breast. If anyone walked in on us, they'd think we'd just made love. But the deal is, I'll lie naked with him if he promises just to caress me. We always end up fighting.

"I meant *the* moment of your life. The moment you realized this is all there is."

I asked my mother the same question once, the summer I came home after Liam died. My mother had just turned fifty, just colored her hair for the first time, a dark red, like the sun setting, and I thought of this as a metaphor because I was young and tragic and reading too much, and all small things had hidden meanings I thought about to make me cry at night, just to make sure I still could.

"The summer I was thirty-eight," she said. "I had my kids half-grown, firm thighs, a new house, and had just learned how to have multiple orgasms."

The summer of my hot pink two-piece.

"I guess I haven't had it yet," I tell Robert.

I finally understand that I was supposed to answer his question with "Right now." As with all things in my life, it comes too late.

He turns his back to me, says "Sorry I'm such a bore."

I sit up, slip on my dress, walk across the room to my boots, stuff my feet into them with a huff and begin lacing them up. I am aware of myself as a beautiful woman, bent at the waist, her hair falling forward, lacing her boots in front of a man who wants nothing more than to grip her small waist as she sits atop him, feel her long hair falling forward around his face.

The first time we undressed and he spread me with his fingers and positioned himself against me and I said no, Robert looked at me like I'd lost my mind.

"You've got to be kidding me," he said, no longer aroused. "I mean, if you don't want to, just say it, but there's no need for such subterfuge."

"How many dead husbands do I have?" I said, holding up three fingers. "Three. Three dead husbands and I saw every one of them go long before they did, and I saw it with them inside of me, and I can't see anything like that again."

Michael, his neck bent against water, its surface as solid as concrete. Liam in his work clothes, flesh on fire, white in hot blue. Like an overexposed photo. Philip hugging a tree, his skin replaced with bark, his arms spindly branches splintered at the elbow. I swear I saw all of it, as clear as day.

When you see these things, you always hope you saw wrong.

All of my husbands came to me like summer. I opened my front door one day and there they were. Michael sketching the lake. Liam cutting the grass at my apartment complex in Athens. Philip stretching his legs on my sidewalk after a run.

Michael and I grew up together in Dade. We were married in my parents' backyard the week after high school graduation and went to college together in Athens, where I studied sociology and he studied business. He snapped his neck jumping drunk off Chimney Rock our junior year, which happens to some kid at least twice a decade.

Liam, a sweet boy I married out of loneliness less than a year after Michael died, fried himself working on power lines. We were married less than six months.

I met Philip, the runner, who had a body like a piston, in my mid-twenties while working at the homeless shelter in Athens. He made cabinets for wealthy people in Atlanta and volunteered for Habitat for Humanity on the weekends, which I also worked with when I could. He fell asleep at the wheel driving back from a job in Rome and slammed into a tree. We were married the longest, just under three years.

I loved them all in a very distant kind of way, although I loved them desperately after their deaths.

I didn't date much after Philip. Three dead husbands isn't much of an advertisement. That is, until I moved back to Dade a year ago and met Robert, who doesn't ask questions about my dead husbands, who cringes when I talk about what I saw with them glistening over me in the night.

Robert, who grew up in Connecticut with his mother but had a father who lived in Montgomery, teaches philosophy at a college up in Georgia, so you'd think he'd be receptive to this kind of thing. My friends who know don't think twice of it, and in fact, my friend Candy (Cane) Robbins jokes that I'm the only mystic atheist she knows.

"If you see things," Robert asked, "Why didn't you warn them?"

"It's not like that," I said. "You don't piece it together until afterwards. And I've never seen anything else, so I wasn't prepared for it. Besides, what am I supposed to warn them against? You can't warn somebody against living."

"Rather inconvenient for them for you to figure it out after the fact," he said.

It took him a few weeks to call me after I told him, but now Robert comes down from Atlanta to fish almost every weekend. He says he's fishing for bass. Big bass. He will stuff them, attach them to beveled, lacquered plaques, hang them in rows on his wall, their mouths open and biting, their feathered gills spread like wings tinged in blood, their spines arched, their tails whipping against air, their bodies gleaming green like his Mercedes. Robert still backlashes on every other throw. Doesn't know what a spinner bait is. Forgets to let out the bilge pump on his expensive Ranger boat, painted in the glittery purple of teenage girls' nail polish.

What Robert's fishing for is his father, who I know from pictures wore a hat and tie and a short-sleeved dress shirt while he fished, right up until the day he died. His father who owned this cabin (Robert gutted it and rebuilt it), but never brought Robert here because Robert preferred books and now feels guilty for his preference. And this I understand: there comes a time in a man's life when truth can be revealed in the translucent, swirled flesh of a plastic fishing worm.

What Robert's fishing for is me, who would be the kind of woman his father wanted for him, the kind of woman who knows how to tie a hook, how to set trotlines, how to spot shad sweeping across water. The kind of woman who pauses for a school of bass dancing silver across the surface of the lake in the same manner most women gawk at diamonds or sunsets on Caribbean Islands.

The lake I live on is in central Alabama, and we got it when they dammed up the Tallapoosa. It has more than 720 miles of shoreline, most of that skinny fingers, but there's plenty of big water for dumb asses from the cities to bring their huge ocean cruisers down and zoom about, at least ten people waving drinks from the overweighted fronts, bikinis and tropical shirts a blur of primary colors. The lake's not made for boats that size, and the rough waters—sometimes with waves the size of a miniature ocean—bite away our seawalls in gaping chunks, like shark bites, if sharks lived in our lake and did things like bite seawalls.

As teenagers, when we didn't worry about the cost of repairs, my friend Candy and I couldn't wait for the summer to come because out-of-town boys with sun-streaked hair and fluorescent Ocean Pacific trunks rolled in with the warm weather. Candy and I put on the tiniest bikinis we could find, sprayed our hair with Sun-In, mixed some baby oil with iodine, slicked ourselves up like bodybuilders, then took the pontoon boat to Chimney Rock to stare at boys through binoculars and watch drunk kids scale the rock to dive off it. Those who lingered earned calls of pussy or city slicker. There were so many boats you could tie yours to the one next to you and by late afternoon have a floating island so large you could be taking tequila shots on a Master Craft ten boats away from your own and never have touched water.

Things are no different now, twenty years later, except the boats have gotten even bigger, the houses on the lake much more ostentatious, some of them in the style of Spanish forts or Tudor homes, the trees on these lots completely cleared, the gaps in the tree line resembling scabs if you're looking from the lake. And the number of people pouring into our town, complaining about the lack of good restaurants or decent grocery stores, has more than tripled. On a Saturday afternoon in July, sitting near the lake is like pulling a lawn chair up to a highway. You can hear nothing but the roar of the boats flitting by dangerously close to shore, dangerously fast.

It's true what they say. Desperation has its own scent. In my town it smells like Aqua Net and perm solution and nail polish and White Shoulders. It my town it smells like shoe polish and Old Spice and gasoline and minnows.

I can say that. I'm from here.

Robert's friends, who are some of the idiots in the ocean cruisers, however, cannot, and it burns me when they come here to enjoy our lake and roll their eyes at the local girls' big hair and cheap clothing, mimic the way we talk, point gleefully at church signs with "Smoking or Non-Smoking?" or "Loving Jesus Isn't a Part-

Time Job," laugh about how there's chitlins in the Pig, like my town's on some nature show on the Discovery channel, except we're in backwoods Alabama and our antiquated, untouched way of living includes huge, honking pickups and shotguns and Bible reading and chitlins in the Piggly Wiggly.

When he brings friends down to fish, I use incorrect grammar to embarrass him. Say fixen. Say ain't. I laugh too loud and wear too tight, too short, too bright clothing. I say cunt. I say cock. I tell them I don't wear underwear and threaten to show them. I drink domestic beer out of the can. Make toasts to the glory of damn rednecks. Tell stories about pissing in Kentucky Fried Chicken parking lots and getting accosted by police. Tell stories about shotgunning beers in the backseats of rusted-out cars. I embellish. Robert puts an arm around my shoulder, whispers in my ear, "What in the hell is your problem? You're acting like a stupid redneck," then laughs for his friends, but makes sure to work into the conversation that I have a degree in sociology from the University of Georgia.

"Hell, what's a degree," I say. "We ain't doing nothing but selling our souls for knowledge." I hold up my beer in another toast, throw back my head, and howl. His friends say things like "Isn't she a card? That Dena, she's something else."

I don't believe that. What I said about school. I love my education. My books. And what I said about souls, I stole that from my mother, and trust me, we got in many fights over her Bible thumping and woe-unto-you speeches.

And usually, when it's just Robert and me lounging around in the sun or fishing from the pier, we don't argue about these things. We talk about poetry and politics. We share anecdotes of youth, ones that don't entail me mud-hopping in a Bronco while smoking pot from a coke can.

Sometimes I think I associate with Robert and his crowd because deep down I agree with them. Maybe I'm embarrassed of how we live here, and like those religious freaks who whip themselves, this is my flailing. Or maybe I'm as vacuous and elitist as Robert's friends, but I get some perverse pleasure in shocking them, which means I'm using the people of my town in a far more insidious way than just for laughs.

I'm eternally conflicted.

For instance, deep down, I'm an atheist. This breaks my heart. Although I was a good Christian girl growing up here, and sometimes I think my mother is right, that I sold my soul for a degree and a few backpacking trips to Europe.

Robert asks me sometimes why I live in such an isolated (that's how he puts it nicely) town if I don't have to. My father's been dead for ten years. My mother went half crazy after he had a stroke and fell off the pier and drowned. Now she lives with my brother Ernie in Tennessee who manages a shirt factory but is trying to start up his own fishing show. He's married to a fat woman named Wilma who has a voice like a hyena and they are crazy for each other and screw like bunnies. But my mother gets along well with them and plans on living out her years there, so there's really no need for me to stay.

I told Robert that I came home from college for my first break hyped up from all the liberal classes I'd been taking. During supper I told my father that capitalism and religion and uneducated people were the scourges of our society. My father nodded, said something about opinions being like assholes, and finished eating his dinner. Later that night I went to the screened-in porch to smoke a cigarette, and my father was sitting there, staring at the lake. "Dena," he said, "do you hate us that much? If I knew I was sending you off to learn to hate where you come from, I'd've kept you here."

"Now do you understand what I'm saying? Why I live here?" I asked Robert.

He didn't.

So I told him that I need to take care of my mother's house, to get it ready to put on the market, although all I've done so far is paint the shutters and plant some azaleas.

Here's what Robert doesn't understand. You could give most of these people a million dollars, and a year later they'd still be living next door to their mommas and grannies and aunts and uncles, still getting in fights over football and women and fishing and Jesus, still want to be buried in the Dade cemetery by the high school, still feeling sorry for people like him.

Here's what Robert doesn't understand. That he's the fool in my town. That the old men at Taylor's Bait Shop tolerate him for my sake. That his expensive boat is an insult to the locals who fish from piers or bridges or old green fiberglass boats with low-powered motors they've rebuilt themselves. That he says crappie wrong. That his crisp khaki vests look silly. That behind his back, they call him a Yankee pussy from Atlanta and I say, *Now boys,* but laugh as loud as the rest of them.

I asked Candy the question Robert asked me, about which moment was *the* moment.

"That's easy," she said, "every time I gave birth."

Candy has five kids and they muscle over her mass like she's a playground slide, run wild, blowing up things with firecrackers and shooting moccasins straight out of the water. She's completely smitten with her husband, Frank, who has an oblong paunch and likes to drink beer and cut up wood with a power saw in the garage on the weekends. Her first husband was six credits short of a degree in English, had a four-inch goatee he swirled around his skinny index finger while he talked, wore leather vests with hand-painted tattoo-like images and silver rings in both ears and on every finger. He'd come to our town for a simpler life but cursed everyone in it for their simplicity. He drove the bookmobile for the local library and would go on long rants about how he was spreading the written word, how he was doing important work, but he was curt and rude to the children who checked out his books. He read Candy poetry in French and whispered Greek myths late into the night, but when she complained that he never made love to her, he told her she'd internalized misogynist concepts of female worth.

"He's gay," I said the first day I met him.

"He's sensitive," she said.

Two years into the marriage he took off with one of his client's fathers to live in a Winnebago in Glacier Park and assemble found poetry from waste left behind by unconscientious campers.

Candy's new husband is amazed by her ability to create a crust for a casserole from Velveeta and Ritz crackers.

"Good God," Robert says when he's at my place and Candy drops by with her brood, "does she have to breed so prolifically?" Candy and Robert have an all-out war going on.

I threw a Memorial Day party this year and invited Robert and several of his friends to join me, Candy and her husband, and my friends from the bait store.

Everybody was just drunk enough, just sober enough, that it was going well, until Candy, whose father died a year ago and so she's still torn up over it, launched into a story about her father's traveling salesman years.

Candy's father, Scooter, drove around the Southeast making calls on factories, touting his Control Central's electronic switches. He was a huge man known for singing when he walked through the town square. It was common practice for salesmen to keep lovers on their sales routes, but Candy's mother was a shrewd woman, and although her head barely reached Scooter's chest, there was no doubt as to who held the power.

I knew how the story went. It was Candy's favorite, happened when she was a little girl. Her father was making a call somewhere in Mississippi. He had a drink in the hotel bar, intending to go to a movie afterward while his buddies entertained their women. In the bar he met another salesman who asked if he could go with Scooter to the movies. On the way home, the man put a hand on Scooter's thigh, asked him to join him for the evening. Scooter, a young man in his twenties, was terrified. When they got back to the hotel, he ran to his room, and the man followed, beating on the door, begging to come in. Scooter, who carried a gun like most men in my town, pulled it out and pointed it where he thought the man's head would be. He called his wife, Millie, with the man still outside beating.

Candy ends the story like this: "Then daddy called my momma, with the guy still out there, and he said, 'Millie, is it legal to shoot queers in Mississippi?'"

Half of the room exploded in laughter. Robert's friends looked mortified. My stomach sank.

"Can you beat that?" Norma said, looking at Robert. "Is it legal to shoot queers in Mississippi?" She slapped her thigh.

Robert dragged me to the kitchen, his whole body shaking.

"That is unacceptable," he said, "You have to ask Candy to leave *now*." He lowered his voice, "My friend, Caleb, is gay. How do you think he feels?"

"Look," I said, rubbing his arm, trying to calm him, "I'm not saying what she said was right. But you call her a redneck practically to her face. So how do you think she feels?"

"Jesus, Dena," he said, "there's your proof right there."

Candy ended up leaving anyway because there was a band at Bill's and she doesn't get out without the kids much and loves to two-step.

And I did talk to her the next day when she dropped by the bait store.

Norma, who was taking inventory in the back, overheard our discussion and started cackling, "Can you shoot queers in Mississippi? I tell you," she screamed from the storeroom, "Candy ought to go on the road."

"Caleb's a sweetie," Candy said, looking truly hurt. "I didn't mean anything by it. That's what happened. Besides," she said, winking, "I love gay men. I was married to one."

This sent Norma into a fit. "I'm telling you," she yelled, "she could pack 'em in."

I tried.

Later the evening of the party, when Robert and I were lying in bed naked and caressing halfheartedly, I suddenly wanted to share something personal with him, make him understand why my friends—who were sometimes racists and ignorant and unforgivable—could at other times bring tears to my eyes. I wanted him to understand how deep they want, how hard they labor, the pleasure they take in telling their stories. How they can be on their way to work at a job where their manager'll fire them for being five minutes late, and they'll pull off the side of the road and take off their caps if a funeral passes, black or white, because they may be ignorant, but they have respect for some things his world couldn't understand.

I tell him about my trip to Horseshoe Bend in fourth grade.

They prepared us in class the week before we went, told us of the battle of Horseshoe Bend at a hoof-shaped turn on the Tallapoosa River in 1814, Andrew Jackson's beginnings as a hero, his winning the bloodiest battle ever fought against the Creek Indians. How blood was spilt on the grassy plains.

They took us there to picnic on those same fields. To watch pretend soldiers dressed in gray and beards, their hands tossing guns like the batons I twirled in gym. To finger fake arrowheads in straw baskets next to the museum information desk. To examine peeling clay statues of brown men painted in the colors of war, frozen in stoic positions behind glass. To straddle dull iron cannons as if they were the grocery store mechanical horses my mother plopped me on to stop my whining.

"Just think," Miss Nichols, my fourth grade teacher whispered, "Indian women and children, huddled along those banks, flailing through that river, like animals, hunching in wet and dark. Can you imagine? One thousand Indians. All that blood. The river red with it."

Later that night, my mother rocked me as I cried. "Why do they tell you such things?" she asked.

Then she told me the truth. How no one died on that morning in 1814. How God saw the surrounded, terrified Indians, and it hurt his heart so, he had the wind whisper to Chief Menawa to ready the women and children. And then the Creeks, all of them, rode the mist of the Tallapoosa to the heavens. Chief Menawa's horse, massive and splendid, had expanded like a storm cloud with God's will and carried the Indians on his back, hundreds, their weight pressing his back right hoof into the soft earth as he jumped to deliverance. The indentation was so severe and yawning that the Tallapoosa tumbled into its depths and forever changed course, wrapping itself in a horseshoe shape near our town in the same manner people tie strings around their fingers. To remind them.

"And I believed her until I had to believe differently," I said. "Although I wouldn't get in water for over a year because of the way the wind rippled the surface. I thought it would take me away. Shoot me to heaven. But isn't that beautiful, what my mother did for me?"

"You should have asked Candy to leave," he said. "It was wrong. You might as well have condoned what she said."

"Did you listen to what I just told you?" I said.

"Yes, your mother rewrote history in order to make it more palatable, minimizing the massacre of one thousand Indians. And I still think that you should have asked her to leave."

"You're missing the point," I said. "What would we do here if we didn't rewrite truth to make it more palatable?"

"You know I'm going to have to call Caleb tomorrow and apologize," he said.

We were lying on my parents' old bed, on the same patchwork quilt comforter I napped on as a teenager in streams of sunshine pouring in from the bay windows my mother had wanted her entire life. Only it was nighttime, the moon huge and smooth, as if someone had cut the heart out of an explosion and slapped it in the sky, and the glow poured over Robert like water. His fists balled. His toes curled. The muscles in his jaw twitched. Winning in his world meant being right.

And I thought, you should ask him to leave.

And I thought, why is he here?

"Come on," I said, sitting up.

"It's two o'clock in the morning," he said.

"Yes," I said, "it's two o'clock in the morning. Now come on."

I put on my boots and stood naked on the back patio waiting for him while he slipped on an undershirt and boxers. I grabbed his hand, laced my fingers through his, and pulled him toward the lake. The frogs bellowed in stereo and the water swayed. It really was beautiful at times like this, when all the skiers and partiers passed out until the next morning when they'd start crawling about at the crack of dawn, hoping to squeeze as much sun and sport out of the day as possible.

We walked though the azaleas I'd planted, their blooms as big as spread-open hands, past the tree I climbed and read in as a teenager to hide from my brother and cousins. I stopped at a leafy patch of earth under a spread of dogwoods.

I dropped to my knees, began clearing the earth of leaves. The soil smelled rich, edible, and I thought of the women my mother told me about, the ones who snuck from their husbands in the middle of night to a patch of earth such as this, to spoon this soil in their mouths by the handful, unable to resist its pull, starved for it.

"You're going to get bugs up you," Robert said. "Some type of infection." He had his arms crossed and was shivering, even though the night hung hot around us. His bald spot shone in the moonlight.

By this time I was sitting on the ground, legs spread, digging in the soil between my thighs. Dirt had worked itself up between my buttocks, and I had a skirt of leaves. I started giggling. I couldn't remember the last time I'd had so much fun. Finally, I saw one slither brown gray, its body stretched long so the ring around its neck looked like a washer under its skin. I snagged it by its slippery end, careful not to tug too hard so it wouldn't break off, its brown insides squirting over my fingers.

"Here," I laughed, dangling the worm in front of my face, smiling up at Robert, who did not look impressed. "This is an earthworm. They don't grow in brown cartons at Norma's store. You should know where they come from."

"Dena," he said, "have you lost your mind?"

"Run inside," I said, "get us a container and we'll dig some up and fish with them tomorrow."

Robert kneeled beside me. He looked concerned. "It's two o'clock in the morning," he said.

And it hit me, just like that: I am thirty-eight. It bolted through me in the same way you sometimes wake disoriented, thinking you're late for an occasion that doesn't exist.

I wondered, has the moment for me passed?

I wondered, is this the moment, and I don't even know it?

"What do you want from me?" Robert asked. The worm pushed against the palm of my closed hand.

This is what I want. To be an oasis of calm. To have candles littered around my house in scents of mango madness and apple euphoria, the names the only hint of chaos. To scatter leather-bound books by Zen gurus or Kant or Aristotle or Plato around my home, and when Robert picks one of them up, I can put my hand warmly on his thigh and say "A book is like a garden carried in the pocket — Chinese Proverb," and have him see a halo of light floating around my enlightened consciousness. I want to wear cowboy boots and cotton dresses, throw away my Mary Kay, rid my cabinets of processed foods crammed with preservatives, live a life of garbanzo beans and tomatoes from my own garden. I want to bake my mother's bread while listening to Johnny Cash with my windows open on Sunday afternoons, to spread homemade honey butter over the thick slices, to drink whiskey out of handmade ceramic cups with my friends from the bait store who I've invited over to share the bread and whiskey and life stories. I want to fold myself into bed at night under my parents' comforter with freshly shaved legs, the rhythm of the lake written in my bones from swimming all day, my cotton dress for the next day draped over the French chair from the eighteenth century I keep meaning to buy, its history of owners known to me and memorized. I want Robert to explain complicated theory to me and for him to still be able to see the beauty in holding a worm you've dug up from your backyard in the palm of your hand, to see the importance in knowing where it came from.

I dropped the worm and recovered the ground with leaves to keep it moist.

"I wanted," I said, "for you to have gotten the container."

Robert asked me to pick up a deli platter from the grocery, and I bring it along with a case of beer and my wave runner to his Labor Day party. After the Memorial Day incident, I had to promise not to pull my redneck act.

When I get there, Robert's grilling hamburgers and Portabella mushrooms on the back porch. Women draped in colorful sarongs dot the pier. The men congregate around Robert in swimming trunks, their milky chests bared. One guy sports a Speedo, which is a first in our town, and I try not to stare. Caleb and another woman from Robert's department tried to swing-dance in the backyard earlier, and he accidentally tossed her into a tree, slicing her lip. She's sashaying around in designer sunglasses with a Band-Aid for a mustache, blending up piña coladas.

By three o'clock we are deliriously drunk on sun and alcohol. A few people are dancing on the pier or splashing in the lake. Robert, Caleb, the Band-Aid lady (whose name is Sherrill), and I are keeping a vigil at the blender. Sherrill, who can barely talk, produces a deck of tarot cards and several candles which insist on blowing out and she insists Caleb relight. She starts giving readings. Caleb might meet a tall dark stranger, but we're not sure since two of his cards fell through the slats of the porch. Robert will come to grips with his Platonist leanings. I will take a trip to unknown lands. I've never seen tarot cards up close before and am awed by the beauty of the images, the heart thrust with three swords, the magician clutching a wand over his head, the hermit, sad and forlorn, his only light a fading lamp.

"You ought to let Dena do that," Robert blurts out. "She *sees* things."

"Really," Sherrill says, offering the deck of cards to me. "Do it up."

"Yeah," Robert slurs, "if she fucks you, she can tell you how you'll go. Pretty high price to pay for a good lay, don't you think?"

"Guess I'll have to find out the old-fashioned way," Caleb says, and Sherrill shrieks.

I close my eyes, put my hands to my temples, say "Let me tell you what I'm seeing right now." I pause for a minute. "Oh, it's coming to me. Yes, I see it. I see that Robert's an asshole."

Everyone laughs. Caleb says, "That Dena, she's something else."

I get up and stalk down to the pier in such a way as to show Robert I'm pissed off. Robert's right behind me. I'm aware of myself as a drunk, half-dressed woman stalking down to my boyfriend's pier with every intention of making a scene. In fact, I already see the scene, a scene that would make Candy proud, the kind of scene you see late at night outside of Bill's in the parking lot. Shrill screaming. Much profanity. Lines like, *I ain't ever wanting to see your face again, you cock sucker, do you hear me! Don't you be messing with me no more!* Motors revving. Tires peeling out. Only I'm on the pier and don't have a car, so I go for the wave runner, but when I attempt to mount the seat, my left foot slips on the wet pier and my arms are reaching for something solid and then my head finds it. Pain splinters my forehead.

This is what I think: how soft the water is. How I forget as an adult to stick my head under and open my eyes. How the water moves so easily to make space for me. How maybe this is my moment, *the* moment, floating here suspended, outside sounds swallowed, the beat of my heart as loud as the frogs bellowing at night in stereo.

This is what I see: my mother smiling from a Styrofoam floating chair, her screwdriver lifted in a toast.

This is what I see: my father sitting on our back porch, staring at the lake as if the answer will wash up to shore.

This is what I see: my brother and cousins, the color of sand and mutts and boys in summer, shimmying their bony hips in my face.

This is what I see: Michael waving after jumping from Chimney Rock, his face golden and content.

This is what I see: Liam taking his boots off in our foyer, his footprints in caked red mud on the welcome mat.

This is what I see: Philip naked to the waist in our backyard at twilight, his hands gliding sandpaper over wood.

This is what I see: the water's surface rippling, the wind carrying it away.

This is what I see: Robert and me atop Chief Menawa's horse, my arms circling his waist, our heads thrown back, both of us howling, the mist from the Tallapoosa lifting us as if we were weightless, the hoof of Chief Menawa's horse pressing into the soil our women spoon into their mouths like manna, the indentation severe and yawning and sure, the river tumbling into it, the new course distinct.

This is what I see: Robert—eyes troubled, arms reaching—his body, smoothed by the water between us, glowing white, like the heart of an explosion, above me.

The Iowa Short Fiction Award and John Simmons Short Fiction Award Winners

2002
Her Kind of Want,
Jennifer S. Davis
The Kind of Things Saints Do,
Laura Valeri

2001
Ticket to Minto: Stories of India and America,
Sohrab Homi Fracis
Fire Road, Donald Anderson

2000
Articles of Faith,
Elizabeth Oness
Troublemakers, John McNally

1999
House Fires,
Nancy Reisman
Out of the Girls' Room and into the Night,
Thisbe Nissen

1998
Friendly Fire,
Kathryn Chetkovich
The River of Lost Voices: Stories from Guatemala,
Mark Brazaitis

1997
Thank You for Being Concerned and Sensitive,
Jim Henry
Within the Lighted City,
Lisa Lenzo

1996
Hints of His Mortality,
David Borofka
Western Electric,
Don Zancanella

1995
Listening to Mozart,
Charles Wyatt
May You Live in Interesting Times,
Tereze Glück

1994
The Good Doctor,
Susan Onthank Mates
Igloo among Palms,
Rod Val Moore

1993
Happiness,
Ann Harleman
Macauley's Thumb,
Lex Williford
Where Love Leaves Us,
Renée Manfredi

1992
My Body to You,
Elizabeth Searle
Imaginary Men,
Enid Shomer

1991
The Ant Generator,
Elizabeth Harris
Traps,
Sondra Spatt Olsen

1990
A Hole in the Language,
Marly Swick

Shannon McCreery

Jennifer S. Davis was born and raised in Alabama, where she grew up exploring the banks of Lake Martin and the Tallapoosa River. In 2001 she received her MFA from the University of Alabama and now lectures at the University of Miami. Her stories have been published in such journals as the *Apalachee Review, Greensboro Review, Hayden's Ferry Review,* and *Crab Orchard Review.*